Freak

F-WORD
BOOK TWO

E. DAVIES

Freak / E. Davies. – 2nd ed.
ISBN: 978-1-912245-20-8

Freak

CHAPTER

One

RIVER

"AND THAT'S WHEN HE TOLD ME HE HAS TO FOCUS ON learning himself. Learn what he wants in a man. Some shit like that."

"Which was right before you caught him leaving with that guy in the gym tank, right?"

"Right." River Connor tipped his head back to finish the dregs of his beer, then sighed and leaned back into the booth. They'd gotten to Woody's early to nab one so they could talk.

"Arrrrgh." Kyle groaned in sympathy for him. He had a man of his own now, but it wasn't that long ago they'd both been convinced they'd never find one.

Well, "not that long" was relative. It felt like ages since they'd been out. They'd both been busy: River hunting for his new job; Kyle setting up Plus's new office, since the charity he worked at had relocated after the fire.

At the office reopening party last weekend, Kyle had cottoned on that there might be someone and had insisted he come find out more.

Unfortunately, things tended to move fast in River's life, and Mr. Maybe Next had become another one-night-stand.

"He was never your type, then, babe. They do that. He was trying you out. Don't let them get to you."

"I knowww," River sighed. "But... *you* know."

"Yeah. Oh, yeah." If anyone understood River's predicament, it was Kyle. Tall, with bright green hair, and gorgeous, he was also femme in the eye-catching kind of way that didn't improve dateability.

They were often seen as easy to spot, easy to fuck, but not boyfriend material. Not discreet, masculine, gym-addicted guys with chiseled jaws and respectable jobs. Not the guy you'd bring home to your parents. Which was a thing they did, because they were the normal kind of gays with families and mortgages—the kind who were only different from the straights because they loved another man.

Not the kind who had to watch their backs walking down dark alleys, who'd abandoned the idea of *family* being about blood, and who loved themselves and each other too fiercely to stay in arbitrary boxes that didn't fit.

River had long ago decided he didn't care about dating, anyway. He lived in the moment.

"Anyway, we need to do this more than once a *month*. Look at you. Get a boyfriend and suddenly forget about me?" River scolded Kyle. Sure, Nic was good for him, but the two of them were lost in each other.

Kyle just laughed. "We'll get more friend time when you're back from the tour," he promised. "The office is almost set up, my crazy overtime is winding up."

"Good." River intended to hold him to that.

"But..."

"You have to get going. Let me guess, your boyfriend's made dinner," River teased. "Or he's done something cute. He sent you a cute selfie. Maybe he's coding something cutely."

Kyle flipped him off. "Fuck off."

"Love you too, babe." River rose to his feet to hug Kyle good night and kissed his cheek, then let him scamper off home.

He was thinking about following, but one more scan of the crowd couldn't hurt. He'd often found the best nights of his life in that one last scan. Also some terrible mistakes when he ran low on options, but…

There. A guy who looked familiar.

Not in the same way as most guys here—even on the outskirts of L.A., every club had its regulars—but something else.

The guy River was watching turned fully to say something to a friend, his profile caught in the light behind the bar, and River's jaw dropped.

Now, that's a blast from the past!

Zeph North. He'd bet his life on it.

And all grown up. Shit, he had muscles now, and his face had filled out around that roguish smile. He carried himself with confidence, not the proactively defensive attitude that he'd once projected.

And he wasn't flirting with that friend, either. Good. Not that River had any right to care, but he couldn't help but wonder… was Zeph single now? What had he been up to in the last five years?

River couldn't stop himself walking over there to find out.

He didn't even have to slow down to pick his way around the couple of narrow tables and pillars in the way. The club was River's stage, even when he wasn't performing here. He knew it better than some of his ex-boyfriends' dicks.

"Zeph North, the man whose name takes longer to pronounce than tying a cherry stem with my tongue."

Zeph's jaw dropped at the sight of him, and then he laughed. "River. Wow. Did you never leave?"

"No. They won't let me go home. But they keep me fed with the only complete protein." Zeph tilted his head, and River winked. "Did you know how many loads it takes per day to meet your caloric—oh! Sorry," River apologized to Zeph's friend, beaming at him. "Where are my manners?"

Zeph's friend was just laughing as he waved off the comment. "A lot?"

"A lot," River agreed, but his gaze was already on Zeph again.

Impossible *not* too look at him, with the clingy white t-shirt showing every fucking ripple of muscle he'd once had and then a lot more. His arms were tattooed now, too—the one he'd had before, plus another across his chest.

River kind of wanted to peel Zeph's clothes off and find out what else was the same.

"You haven't changed a bit," Zeph murmured, raising a brow. Just like old times, the expression felt like a challenge to River, who had to fight back the urge to respond in kind.

"Thanks." River leaned his hip against the table. "How did the move go? What have you been up to? We should catch up."

"Yeah." Zeph gave him one of those rare full smiles—or rare back then, at least. River hoped for his sake that he was happier now. When Zeph stretched out a hand for his phone, River dug it out, unlocked it, and opened a new contact while accepting Zeph's phone in return.

He had to scroll past the useless recently-used emoji section to add a kissing emoji to his name after he typed it in. That was a good sign, right? But Zeph wasn't the type to flirt by emoji anyway.

Again, River had to remind himself, *hadn't been.*

He'd hardly known Zeph back then, let alone now.

Maybe it was the thrill of the chase, but when they handed back each other's phones and their hands brushed, River felt a shiver down his spine.

Since Zeph was out with a friend, he'd leave him be... for tonight. With his phone number now, River had plenty of time to get him warmed up by text.

"Perfect." River pocketed his phone, winked, then blew a kiss at them both. "Don't let me keep you. Bye, darling."

He swanned off to the other side of the room without looking back, but he felt Zeph's eyes on him as keenly as he always had. When Zeph looked away, he knew because the tingle of being watched faded.

Jesus. Just like old times indeed.

It felt like Zeph's finger brushing lightly down his spine, from the back of his neck all the way down to his ass, promising... ecstasy. Promising those strong arms around him, the strong lips against his...

And River was horny now. He ducked out of the club without even saying good night to anyone, striding down the street toward his place. Halfway there, he got a text.

Great seeing you. Let me know how you've been.

River didn't need a guy by his side tonight. Not with the

vivid memory of Zeph buried deep inside River, his legs wrapped around his waist as Zeph fucked him against the glass shower wall.

River needed a hot shower and a few minutes alone before he could even *think* of answering that text.

CHAPTER
Two

ZEPH

"Let me guess: you fucked him."

Zeph's brows drew together as he looked back at Tristan over the newly-opened bottles of beer. "Actually, we dated."

Tristan's surprise was easy to read. His friend was expressive, which was why he'd done so damn well in show biz, but so poorly dating. "Oh. You never said," Tristan murmured, looking after River, but River was gone.

Zeph didn't bother trying to find him. For all River could catch and hold a room's attention, when he didn't want to be seen, he could move his ass. And he knew River just well enough to know that he'd been giving Zeph a taste of him.

He'd sent a quick text while he ordered at the bar, but he didn't expect to hear back tonight. Actually, Zeph kind of hoped he wouldn't. Normally he'd be up for an easy fling, but tonight was about Tristan.

It was true, he hadn't told Tristan, or anyone, about River. But he didn't have a lot of friends apart from Tristan. Some at the gym, some in the sport or in the ring, but not close friends.

When a guy like Tristan went through a rough breakup, Zeph was willing to drop anything to be with him for a night and make sure he was okay—really okay, not just fake-okay.

"Hey, don't make this about me," Zeph teased. "Tonight is cheer-you-up night. And besides, we weren't serious. Not like you and—"

Tristan raised a finger and Zeph trailed off. His lips were pinched, his fingers curled tightly around the bottle. "Tell me about him."

Zeph paused. "Oh, man." This wasn't his strong suit. "You need the distraction that bad, huh?"

"It's this or about a dozen more of these," Tristan raised his bottle, "and I don't wanna be pissing all night. Oh, God. If I get caught in the men's bathroom here…"

Zeph rolled his eyes. "They don't blog about every man who takes a leak in a gay bar in the Gay Times, you know."

Tristan narrowed his eyes and pointed the neck of his bottle at Zeph. "You're deflecting."

"So are you."

Tristan shrugged and stubbornly stared Zeph down. Even though Zeph faced worse in the cage every fucking fight, he didn't want that kind of tension, so he scoffed and threw up his hands. "Fine, you win."

"Where'd you meet?"

"Here."

"This exact bar?" Tristan exclaimed. "Dude, coincidence."

"Don't get on me with your Hollywood hippie, granola-crunching, *law of attraction* stuff," Zeph warned instantly, grinning at him. "But yeah, here. When I lived here, right before I moved out to the Midwest for training. We dated for a week. It was literally the week before I got the offer from my first gym."

"Ohhh. Shit," Tristan breathed out. "You never said you left someone behind."

"No, because we weren't yet… you know."

Tristan nodded. "Gotcha. A week in. Pretty new."

"Yep."

"You're still into him." Tristan's eyes sparkled with mischief now.

"Oh, God. Here we go."

Tristan laughed. "I'm not saying pick rings now. But he's your type, isn't he? All… out there, and stuff. And you've been single, *focusing on your career*, for how many years now?"

"Ugh." Zeph waved him off. Tristan was right, sadly.

"Think of your dick."

"I do. A lot. We have a rapport. It's only boyfriends I don't do," Zeph assured him. "Think I'm letting these guns go to waste?" He flexed for Tristan's benefit.

"Jesus, you got an ego while you were gone," Tristan laughed. "Speaking of which, when's your next fight? How's that going?"

Zeph grimaced. There was a mood-killer. He folded his arms against the table again. "Couple months away. But it's getting tougher. I'm not getting younger."

"I feel you there, man." Tristan tapped his bottle against Zeph's and drank.

Zeph rolled his eyes. "I know you're barely thirty, because I am, too."

"Exactly," Tristan said. "Too old to play high school or college… too young to play the serious parts…"

"Isn't that prime love-interest range?" Zeph asked.

Tristan leaned in. "Yep. Which is exactly why I need to be

further in the closet than… I don't know… Marlon Brando. James Dean. You know?"

Zeph let it go for now, but eyed Tristan to make it clear the subject wasn't closed. "So we're both in that not-middle-aged, not-young-adult stage."

"That's gotta be harder in the MMA scene, though." Tristan frowned. "Don't fighters start retiring?"

"The bad ones do. The good ones have a name, or they've been training for long enough that they can last longer."

"You're pretty good, though, aren't you?"

Zeph chuckled. "Oh, you flatter me. I started at twenty-five. Dude, that's *old*."

"Oh." Tristan frowned. "So what's next? Is it time for a change?"

"I don't know. I'm not prestigious enough to be a trainer. I win fights, but not enough, and not fast enough. It's only a few per year. That's why you get such a head start if you start young."

Zeph tried to quell the frustration deep in his gut with another swig of beer, then rolled his head back.

If he had anyone else to fall back on, things would be easier. Family, close friends, just anyone with a need for a gnarly-looking guy without any real talents.

Tristan kicked him. "Hey, man. At least you didn't just get dumped—again—because you're not willing to look at every casting agent's couch from now on and wonder whose dick you're gonna have to suck."

"It's not like that, I'm sure," Zeph scoffed. "Come on."

Tristan shrugged. "Safer not to find out."

"Look at us," Zeph laughed, rubbing a hand down his arm and over the rosary tattoo there. It was an instinctive gesture by now, engrained in him. "Doing a great job being the sad assholes in the corner."

"Well, your asshole might be a lot happier if you'd followed that River guy—"

Zeph snorted with laughter and almost sprayed his beer over Tristan's face.

"Ew."

"Serves you right," Zeph told him. "You saw me drinking there and went for it anyway."

But they were both grinning as they settled back. Even if their minds weren't at ease, they at least had this bond of friendship. A couple of beers and a good conversation were always something to fall back on.

And that wasn't nothing. Far from it. Friends were hard to find, and harder to keep.

CHAPTER
Three

RIVER

"AMAZING WORK, EVERYBODY! YOU LOOKED *STUNNING*, courtesy me..."

"Oh, pat yourself on the back later." Tina Spirit grinned across the room at River. She slid her wig off and grabbed makeup wipes.

"I will," River grinned. "But you sounded great, too. So take the fucking compliment."

"Consider it taken!" called Glam Ritz, one of his closest friends. She was leaning back in her chair, tugging off one high-heeled boot at a time. "What a show."

River blew out a sigh. That was an understatement. They deserved to celebrate pulling this one off.

It wasn't a *bad* performance, by any means. Just the front of the house got a little rough and rowdy, and security weren't able to step in without breaking up the mood.

So it had been up to the queens to do it, and being the professional performers they all were—even though nearly all of them were amateurs, since there was no money in drag outside the top echelon—they handled it fine.

"That reminds me, though," River frowned. "How are we going to handle that if it comes up in Ginny's? Or Vegas?"

About half the girls in this one-off show were also in the upcoming tour they were doing, spending two nights in L.A. before driving to Vegas for eight performances over ten days at several different bars.

"We'll handle it however we can. Let Glam throw them out the door if we have to."

Glam flexed a bicep and unzipped her dress. "I won't even break a nail, honey. But we should think about security."

"A man we can trust to take on the road with us?"

"No, a man we can trust each other not to *take* on the road..." Candy spoke up. Also known as RB, Candy was one of River's closest friends in the scene, and in general.

Guffaws and titters swept the room.

"Where do you find an ugly bouncer? A straight bar?"

They were all laughing now.

Across the room, Jizzie Bell shrugged. "I dunno. I haven't been to one in *years*, honey. I doubt if any of us have! Anyone?"

"Actually..." River hummed, an idea popping into his head.

RB nearly fell off his stool as he tugged his jeans up. "Shit. You're switching teams and you didn't even tell me?"

"No, no, no," River snorted with laughter. Of all the ladies and gentlemen here, he was among the least likely to enter a straight bar without serious bribery. "But I know someone."

"Someone ugly? Oh, baby, we don't need any of your sloppy seconds around."

River flipped off the speaker and went on. "An MMA fighter I know. But I don't know if he'd be up for it."

"Lordy." RB grinned at him. "Now you have my attention again. All of it."

"Can we bribe him? Or pay him? What's the going rate for—you never said if he was ugly. We should establish this first," Jizzie piped up.

River laughed. "He isn't, okay?"

"He isn't ugly?"

River threw up his hands. "Don't you want to know if he's a good fighter? Lord almighty, your priorities." But he couldn't stop laughing, even as he said it.

"Show us."

"His fights?"

"No, his Facebook. Do we know him?" Three or four of them swarmed River. It didn't take much poking and prompting before he groaned and dragged out his phone to call up Zeph's minimalist Facebook profile.

"Ohhhh. He's *gorgeous*. Come on, call him up. Ask him."

"See what rate he wants, and we'll see what we can do. What's the going rate for a trick? Between all of us..." RB trailed off.

River elbowed RB and called him. "Jesus, pipe down, then." He held out his hand and lowered it, the universal backstage signal for *volume down*.

Everyone obeyed, although some were still giggling to each other quietly.

The phone went to voicemail. Damn it.

But that was just as well. Trying to hold a business conversation—or something like it—with all of his friends around? Nearly impossible, he was sure.

"Hey, Zeph."

He heard the whispers of Zeph's name between each other as they checked their memories to see who might know him. Luckily, nobody looked suddenly interested or stunned. Didn't mean someone hadn't forgotten his name, but it was a weird, memorable one, at least. Not like James, or Ben, or something like that. The "one degree of separation" rule among gay men was more like two or three in L.A., thank God.

"It's River. Good seeing you the other day. I have a business proposition for you. Call me back when you have a minute and maybe we can work something out. Okay, bye." River always pitched up his voice on the phone, and he drawled out the last syllable before he hung up.

"Ooooh. Someone's flirting."

River pointed his phone at Glam. "*You're* flirting. With everyone in that crowd. The guy you gave the lap dance to? He was wrapped around your pinky. Good lord, woman. You *have* a perfectly functional boyfriend—as far as I'm aware..."

"Oh, but he's getting boring," Glam sighed dramatically, shrugging on her little denim jacket. "Or bored of me, more to the point. I think I'll have to upgrade."

That turned the attention onto her—sympathies, people offering to slap her boyfriend or set her up with someone they knew, etc—and off River, thankfully. River wasn't quite sure he knew how to answer them if they insisted on finding out how they knew each other.

Zeph *was* the perfect guy for the job. Of anyone they knew, he was most likely to accept drag wages, or some form of payment in lieu of money. And he was smart, strong, protective, well-trained... he wouldn't disrupt the crowd needlessly.

Despite dating him for just a week and a half five years ago, River had gotten to know him well enough to trust him in a bad situation.

Throughout drinks with his friends, and on the way home afterward, River kept his phone in his hand so he didn't miss the return call. And when he settled down to sleep, he plugged it in and set it next to his pillow.

Just for old time's sake, it would be nice to see Zeph again for longer than a couple of minutes.

Really, really nice.

CHAPTER
Four

ZEPH

MMA FIGHTERS WEREN'T MACHINES; NOR WERE THEY animals. They weren't showmen faking hits and diving. Whatever people's perceptions, Zeph always insisted that they were trained athletes, and one glimpse at his grueling schedule took them aback.

He had to watch what he ate, and when and how he worked out. At times, he trained from dawn 'til dusk in one way or another. Mental and physical focus both took work to improve, and knowledge of the opponent's style was hard-won through watching old tapes of them. Plus, Zeph had long since grown accustomed to pre-dawn runs, and maintaining a rigorous bedtime routine helped get him out of bed in the morning.

During peak training periods, he would cut off literally any conversation at eight PM to start his bedtime routine. He wasn't currently in the peak period—not quite yet, not for another few weeks—but he still maintained those habits in the off-time.

Part of taking care of his body was ensuring no exposure

to electronic screens for the last hour before bedtime. He also didn't have a lot of people who were close to him. A couple of friends, really, and some online friends who knew how to email him.

It made sense to shut off his phone before he started his bedtime routine, therefore, and Zeph didn't turn it on again until after his morning run, protein shake, weight routine, shower, and breakfast—nearly always in that order.

The voicemail notification, therefore, took him by surprise.

He raised the phone to his ear to listen as he rinsed the last few dishes. He paused, setting the last pot in the drain tray and towelling off his hands when he recognized a voice.

It was River.

Call me back when you have a minute...

Zeph focused on River's words. There was a little flirtation there, sure, but he was pretty sure it was a genuine business proposal.

Well, if River wanted him to dress in drag, he was going to have to turn him down. Zeph was pretty sure nothing River fit into would look cute on him.

He got River's voicemail in return.

"Hey River, it's Zeph." He quickly glanced at the clock. When he woke early, even after his routine was complete, he was sometimes up and moving before seven. To most people, that was hellishly early.

Phew. It was almost eight. Almost normal.

"I got your call. Uh, I guess we're playing telephone tag now. Call me back, if you've still got that business proposition to talk about."

It wasn't even a minute before his phone rang. River.

"Hey, Zeph. Glad you called."

He caught himself thinking River's sleepy voice was cute. Scratchy but warm. He could hear the smile. "Uh, you too? What's up?"

"Can we meet up? Brunch somewhere?" River suggested.

Visions of fifteen-dollar strawberry mimosas danced in front of Zeph's eyes. That was the other thing—MMA fighters, unless they were in the top tier or they had a *lot* of fights, weren't millionaires. Sponsorship paid, but again, the top tier got those offers.

"Where?" he cautiously asked. "Uh, I just ate, but I can have something." He was a little short on protein. Scrambled eggs or something wouldn't kill him.

Oh, yeah. It was Saturday. Cheat day! French toast it was.

"I know a great, cheap little place. It's a little hole-in-the-wall. Iggy's."

"Perfect." Zeph glanced down at himself. He'd just changed, but he'd chosen sweatpants and an old, comfy t-shirt today. He'd have to wear something nicer if he was about to meet River. "That'll take me, like, twenty minutes or something."

"No worries." River yawned on the other end of the phone. "I gotta—I gotta get up and stuff."

Zeph smiled. He'd only woken up beside River a couple of times, but he remembered how slow River was to wake. It was adorable.

Again with that. Knock it off. Exes are exes, he reminded himself.

"Sure. No rush. Show up when you show. Whoever gets there first grabs a table." Zeph shrugged out of his old t-shirt and into a nice, tight new one. He chose dark jeans that made his ass look good.

"Perfect. See you in a few," River told him, running water in the background. "If I don't fall asleep at the coffee pot."

"Reassuring. Wait, coffee—we'll get it at the place."

"Silly. Coffee to get me *to* the place," River teased.

Zeph minimized his caffeine intake. Another fun part of being an athlete—the caffeine-free green teas when whoever he was out with guzzled fatty lattes. "Oh. Yeah. Late night?"

"Not as late as I'd like." That was definitely flirtation in River's voice.

Zeph chuckled as he pulled his shoes on, then patted his pockets. "Okay. I'm on my way out. Catch you in a couple."

"Sweet lord almighty, give me a chance to catch up here."

"I'll give you a head start, then. I won't even drive."

"Or run."

"Or run," Zeph promised, his lips twitching into a smile as he locked his front door.

"Like that helps," River muttered. "Where's my... where's... I left... right..." he mumbled to himself. "Christ on a cracker, you could walk backward and beat me there. I don't even have pants on."

Zeph couldn't refrain from grinning now. "Oh? What else are you wearing?"

"Hey," River's laugh was sharp but playful. "Wait and find out."

"Don't make me wait too long. Not sure I can handle blue balls this early. Bye." Zeph hung up and grinned at his phone, picturing the look on River's face. If River was still River, that would get him there at least ten minutes faster.

Sure enough, Zeph had only just gotten his unsweetened iced tea when River stumbled through the diner door, blinking and scanning the room slowly.

River always strode so tall and confident, like he knew exactly where he was going and would stomp a three-inch high heel through the foot of anyone in the way. But he looked adorable right now half-asleep, clinging to the doorframe and shielding his eyes. He'd dressed down in skinny black jeans, red Converse, and a lacy black butterfly dress.

Zeph was pretty sure he could see River's nipples from here.

His lips twitched into a smile. He raised a hand to catch River's eye, then waited as the blond made his way over. Zeph couldn't help but notice he'd styled his hair, too, despite how half-asleep he looked.

"Morning," River grumbled. "If it counts as that yet."

"It's not even nine," Zeph told him, grinning. "I got you out of bed *real* early. Must be one hell of a business proposition."

River sighed dramatically. "Leaving bed early doesn't happen unless he's got an over thirty-degree bend in his—morning, darling. Black coffee." He blew the waitress a kiss of appreciation with both sets of fingertips, and she grinned back.

He was a regular here, then. Zeph wasn't surprised. He glanced back at River, his brows rising. "Getting back to thirty-degree bends...?"

"Come on. You're telling me you've never had a fishhook dick."

The name made Zeph cringe, curling his toes into his shoes.

"Yeah. Exactly." The waitress—Tasha, her name tag read—

brought River a cup and he kissed her cheek. "You're a life-saver. How'd the birthday party go?"

Tasha sighed with what sounded like relief, pushing her hair back up in the bun and twisting it around the pencil again. "She was good as gold. Coloring books. Who knew?"

"The old ways are the best," River nodded, flashing her a grin and sipping his coffee. "I found a couple good-as-new books at the Sally Ann, actually. I'll bring by the nature one for her."

"Oh, that's so sweet!" A smile bubbled across Tasha's face. "Haley's gonna love that."

"Next time my brain's functional," River promised. "I'll drop it off this afternoon. I'm saving the princess one for Kevin." He glanced at Zeph. "Kyle's kid."

Zeph nodded like he knew who Kyle was, searching his memory. Had he met him? He couldn't remember meeting any of River's friends.

Tasha's curious gaze was on him now, and Zeph did his best to meet it with a friendly smile and nod.

This was classic River—knowing everyone, taking care of the people around him… but was he looking after himself? He'd always pretended to put himself first, and sneakily helped everyone else.

A bell rang on the kitchen and Tasha turned to grab her next order. "Oops. Talk to you later, hon."

River blew a kiss at her retreating back, then stretched out in the booth, slipping a compact mirror out of his pocket and flipping it open to check his lips. Was he wearing gloss? Zeph couldn't tell. His lips *did* look kind of one matte color all over, now that he thought about it.

"Where were we?" River hummed, tapping one slender finger against his lips.

Zeph tried *hard* not to remember those fingers curled around his cock, those pretty lips pursing around the head of his cock.

Oh, God, did he remember the sex. They'd always been good in bed. That whole week and a half of dating, that had gone *well*.

"Right! Business." River straightened up, his thumb grazing the edges of his nails as he idly glanced down at them. "Are you busy for the next couple weeks?"

"Er... Busy how?" Zeph straightened up to mirror the pose, smoothing his t-shirt down as if he were about to interview for a damn job.

"Mm." River gave him a quick appreciative glance up and down, tilting his head.

Oops. Zeph realized the t-shirt *was* a little small for his size right now.

River's gaze was on his face again, his eyes sparkling with mischief. "How'd you like a little easy security job on the road?"

There was a lot to unpick there. Zeph paused. "Security?"

"My drag show. Not *my*, but I'm doing it with a few of the other girls. A dozen of us. We're doing tonight and tomorrow night here in L.A., then ten days in Vegas."

Zeph nodded slowly, seeing where this was going.

"And we had a few hecklers, a few rowdy obnoxious guys in the front last night. We handled it, but... you know. It'd make us more comfortable to have someone we know is on our side, not the bar's side."

"There's a difference?"

"The bar likes large groups of frat boys who buy a shit-ton of drinks." River pursed his lips, then shook his head and flipped open his menu. He instantly flipped it shut and put it down. "Oh, why bother? I know what I'm having."

"What's that?"

"Belgian waffle, all the toppings."

Oh, God. That sounded *incredible*.

Cheat day, Zeph reminded himself. And the last few weeks, he hadn't even really cheated. He was getting boring.

"Even whipped cream…" River teased, his voice low.

Zeph's gaze snapped up to River's face, but River wasn't flicking his tongue out in that dirty, suggestive way. Christ, if he was flirting, he was playing this one slowly. Zeph decided to gloss over the comment. "I'll have that, too. So, the payment terms?"

"That… would be the sticky part."

"Hopefully literally." Zeph couldn't resist the immature comment. River brought it out in everyone he was around if they were so inclined to think that way. And it was a relief to be as fucking gay as he wanted without a side-eye like he sometimes got from the gym bros.

River winked. "We can cater to those terms. But not many others. We can do… maybe a couple hundred bucks, or a cut of the tips, but that's dicey for us all. And for Vegas, we can carpool. I'll pay for gas if you drive, or I'll drive us. And you can share a room with one of us—probably me, since we…"

"Yeah. Know each other."

"*Know* each other," River echoed, and to his credit, he only slightly drawled the first word, though he was smirking as he sipped his coffee. "And we'll cover food, too. Basically, free Vegas trip. I know there's fights there you could see."

That was exactly where Zeph's mind had gone, right after he'd ripped it away from the image of them sharing a cheap hotel room.

He wasn't sure exactly who was fighting there, but there was bound to be someone. At the very least, he could drop by the local gyms.

In his position, looking for training jobs he hadn't really earned, he couldn't turn down the chance to network. A bit of gambling money, memorable times with River and his ever-interesting circle of friends, maybe a favor or two if the mood was right…

What the hell? Zeph had nothing to lose.

"Yeah. I'll do it."

CHAPTER
Five

RIVER

THERE WAS NOTHING LESS FUN THAN TRYING TO GIVE ANOTHER girl a last coat of mascara while shimmying into his own dress. Makeup had a way of getting everywhere it shouldn't if he wasn't paying very close attention to it. River habitually arrived early at any show he worked. Even more so with this tour, since he was wearing both hats—makeup artist and performer—not even counting the frankly adorable hat in one of his numbers.

When he approached the steel back door of the club where they'd been lucky enough to get a stage all weekend, Zeph was waiting next to it, hands in his pockets, disappearing into one of those giant, warm hoodies of his.

River smiled fondly. It brought back a moment's remembrance of their past together.

For once, the relationship had been short and sweet, with no hard feelings when it ended. Though Zeph had been the one leaving, it had suited River to break up when they did, too. Right when it was getting to that uncomfortable *feelings* stage. He'd had the feeling Zeph was feeling about the same.

"Hey." Zeph pulled one hand out of the kangaroo pocket of his hoodie and waved loosely at him. "I guess I found the place."

River grinned. "Yep. Great job, Holmes."

"Are you Watson or Moriarty?"

River batted his lashes as he slid past Zeph, their shoulders brushing, and pulled open the door to the club. "Depends on my mood that night."

He heard Zeph catch his breath. His ex murmured back, "What about tonight?"

"Can't a guy be a little of both?" River smoothed a hand down his front to indicate the double entendre, adjusting the bag on his shoulder.

Zeph's lips tugged up in a smile. He nodded slightly. "If you like."

Even back then, he'd known he was interested in drag, and though not a woman, not particularly interested in being the definition of a man. Zeph's easy acceptance of that years ago had taken River aback.

A fair number of guys who looked like Zeph were allergic to femmes, fags, and flaming homos like him. Pull out a compact to touch up and they'd react like you were cradling a tarantula. River still knew Zeph would screw up sometime, especially in this kind of atmosphere, but his heart was in the right place.

They'd had a few conversations back then about it—about River's fondness for skirts and men's shirts, wigs, and full-face makeup both in everyday life and in the club. Zeph had seemed determined to understand, even if he couldn't quite do so.

The club didn't open for another half hour, giving him plenty of time to introduce Zeph to the bartenders and club security; the bartenders were a good first point of contact for a problem patron without obviously summoning security.

"You ready for this?" When Zeph nodded, River led him over to do exactly that.

Sebastian and Gino were behind the bar tonight—a pair of gorgeous Italians. One was short and blond and one tall and dark. A surprising number of bartenders at gay clubs were open-minded straight guys willing to milk their abs for tips, but these two were a couple.

And yeah, River had been in the middle of *that* sandwich once or twice.

He draped himself against the counter. "Hey, handsome," he chirped. He blew Sebastian a kiss and waved down at Gino at the other end of the bar.

"Hey again," Sebastian grinned, his gaze flickering to Zeph. The up-and-down glance wasn't hard to notice. "And who have you brought to flirt with me tonight?"

"Zeph North. A friend of mine, MMA fighter, all-around badass. We—the queens—are hiring him as personal security for when we go to Vegas."

"MMA. Wow," Sebastian whistled under his breath, and River felt a weird moment of pride.

Zeph brushed it off humbly, as usual, by waving a hand. "The equivalent of a mid-lister," he told Sebastian. He wasn't hitting on him? Weird. Everyone hit on Sebastian, and Sebastian was the closest to River in type...

Gino came over to interrupt the fuss. "I have a friend who's really into MMA! Real gym bunny. Wait 'til I tell him about this."

"You want a picture or something?" Zeph grinned.

Gino crowed, "Fuck, yeah. He'll *hate* me."

"When you say *friend*…" River teased, flicking his tongue out playfully.

Sebastian rolled his eyes, watching Zeph lean against the counter and flash the phone camera a big grin. "He's always trying to… warm him up." The Italian accent was soft on his tongue, but it was pleasing to the ear. So distracting.

"With hate." River offered a broad grin. "It works."

"It works," Sebastian murmured, winking at him. The two of them certainly remembered their night together, then. His gaze flickered to Zeph, back to River, and he raised an eyebrow.

River drew a breath and shook his head slightly, but something in his expression made Sebastian raise an eyebrow instead of accepting his answer.

"Oh, there's Reg. C'mon. Stop playing celebrity," he teased, hooking his finger into the pocket of Zeph's hoodie and leading him over to the doors.

Reg greeted him with a laugh. "Found yourself a boy toy?"

"Fuck off." River flipped Reg off, but he smirked.

"Oh, a friend?" Reg looked sheepish for a moment, then offered Zeph a hand. "I assumed…"

"It *is* River." Zeph flashed him a teasing look. "I'm glad he hasn't changed that much."

The two were similar in size and build. They did that alpha male "sizing each other up" look while they shook hands with a firm pump of flesh on flesh.

"You knew each other before?"

"Yeah, years ago. I'm back in town now."

"And," River interjected before it could get all awkward, "our hired security for the queens for the rest of the tour."

Reg looked concerned, turning toward him now. "Did it

shake you that much last night? Dixie gave the all-clear signal—"

"No, no, darling." He wrapped his arm around Reg's shoulder and kissed his cheek. Normally he towered over the man, but he was in Converse today. River didn't want him to feel bad. He was exactly right—the queens had decided to handle the crowd themselves.

"Okay. But if you need more backup…"

"That's why we have another big tattooed man of our own now." River seamlessly transferred his hold to Zeph, draping his arm around his neck.

Heat crackled between them, and it felt just like old times for half a second. He pulled his arm away.

"That and eye candy."

"You didn't tell me that," Zeph accused him, but he was playfully smiling.

"Oops." River gave him an unrepentant smile. "Then, you —Reg—can keep more of a general eye on the place, and Zeph can look all muscly and keep the drunk assholes from actually trying to take the stage."

Reg nodded briskly. "Great. All right. I gotta grab the ID machine, so—"

"Yep. I'll get dressed." River fluttered his fingers in a wave to both of them, leaving Zeph to wander the club and talk to the staff while he made his way to the staff room-cum-dressing room.

The costumes were carefully planned for as little on-and-off as possible. That meant sheer tights first, then bright purple fishnets—at a distance, nobody could see it wasn't bare skin. Over that went a plaid skirt and halter top.

His wig was already mostly ready, so it didn't take long before he had the pigtails looking just right.

The makeup was the last part, and only now did he notice Zeph flitting in and out of the room. He'd taken off his hoodie and was in a tight black shirt now. Second-best thing to a tight white t-shirt on him.

River had no complaints about it, but he felt Zeph watching while he pressed his brush into the setting powder, layering a sheer, youthful look before picking his bright red lipstick.

Zeph had watched him put on makeup in his bathroom before, all those years ago. He couldn't figure out how it made him feel to have Zeph watching him again now.

So much had changed, and yet… so little had.

"Oh, now she's making us all look bad."

River blew a kiss at a few of his friends as they entered. RB, Dixie, and Glam had carpooled, and they brought the room to life as soon as they were in it.

River was *alive* again, his body remembering the pre-show adrenaline rush it was supposed to get swept away in. He started flitting between them to catch up on their Saturdays while they dressed.

If he had a closest friend apart from Kyle, it was probably RB. His full name was Rene Boswell, but he absolutely hated it, and River was one of the few who actually knew what it was.

He preferred RB outside drag. In drag, she was Candy Came.

RB waited until Zeph wandered out of the room again, then stage-whispered, "Did you *see* the security they got? That's Zeph, isn't it, River?"

Most queens opted for *she* but RB usually used *they* pronouns for River when he was in drag. RB knew him better than most people—well enough to know that River didn't care about pronouns.

Just because he was used to it, River thought of himself as *he* most of the time, but he liked that Kyle and RB went neutral with him sometimes, especially while he was in drag. It was a nod to the part of him that just wasn't attached to gender. Using *she* pronouns while in drag was standard in drag scenes, but it just wasn't him the rest of the time.

Honestly, all pronouns felt a little like a lumpy old college sweatshirt that was made for people with really short torsos and unnaturally long arms, and never fit quite right.

River giggled as he came over to tug RB's zipper up and pin it. "I thought I'd introduce you all at once."

"Oh, no, mister. No holding out on us." Zeph stepped back into the room and RB clicked his tongue, waving to get his attention. "*Hello!* You must be the nice man who's keeping the not-so-nice men off our stage."

"That's me," Zeph agreed with that heartwarming, slow, gleaming smile. Sometimes with that smile and his laidback drawl, he showed a hint of southern influence, but he didn't have the accent the rest of the time. River couldn't remember where he'd spent the most time. All Zeph had said was that he'd moved around a lot.

"Well, *hello.*" RB offered his hand for Zeph to kiss, and suddenly everyone wanted that.

River fought back a smile as he brushed a touch-up of eyeshadow across Glam's upper lid. "Oh, hold on," he tutted as she tried to wiggle away and join the greetings.

The other queens were arriving and joining in the introductions, and the sexual, flirtatious energy was downright impossible even for the most clueless bystander to miss.

Dixie was draped around him, squeezing his biceps while

she examined his tattoos, and RB perched on a stool in front of him, suspiciously close to crotch level.

Everyone ogling Zeph at once made River... well. He couldn't quite figure out what was going on, but it seemed a hell of a lot like jealousy. He finished with Glam and waved her off to meet Zeph, then went to help Tina with a spot of clear nail polish to fix the run before it was an emergency.

The atmosphere backstage was always friendly and buzzing. Especially in a tight knit group like theirs, there wasn't room for drama or jealousy. There could be catfights and bitter rivalries in the scene, but this little part of the L.A. scene was mutually supportive, for the most part.

River glanced back and bristled when he saw Glam patting Zeph's chest, giggling with the others about the MMA training routine he was describing.

It *was* jealousy. That was *his* Zeph. They could look, but he hadn't told them they could touch.

What the fuck?

That thought was so abnormal for him he actually stopped, brush halfway into the polish, before he shook off the thought.

"Something the matter?" Tina tilted her head, then checked her wig to make sure it was staying in place.

"No. Just thought of something. It can wait."

And that it could. This was just business. They weren't *together*, River reminded himself as he blew on the polish, waiting for it to dry and testing it with a fingertip now and then.

Sort of. I mean, we can't ignore that flirting earlier today... Even on the way into the club, if he really thought about it. But there was no time to think about it. They had to go over the schedule again, make absolutely sure everyone knew their cues.

The show was supposed to start ten minutes ago, which meant they should start sometime in the next twenty minutes, and Fanny Delite had forgotten her boobs, so they were scrambling to find the right size between everyone else's spares. Plus, River ticked off on his fingers, someone had to run the CD to the DJ...

They barely had enough time to take care of the last-minute tasks, let alone thoughts like those. River firmly set them aside.

It's showtime.

CHAPTER

Six

ZEPH

ZEPH HAD BEEN HESITANT TO LET PEOPLE INTO HIS LIFE SINCE he was seven, standing on the step of his first foster home and still trying to understand that he was an orphan now.

This job, though? It was nice. The queens were genuinely sweet to one another and him, and he could tell that the comments that sounded catty to him at first hid a deep affection for one another. It wasn't unlike his own friends in the gym, who he sometimes sparred with, sometimes fought with for money, sometimes shot cheap jabs at while training, but would do anything for.

Hanging out with the queens might not pay well, but it was one of the easiest jobs Zeph had done. And, honestly, the attention from them wasn't an unwelcome ego boost. He liked being a protector for them.

Still, Zeph didn't relax until Sunday night.

The first night was learning the routine—staying out of the way of queens hustling between the makeshift dressing room, when the queens didn't mind audience members pushing singles into their bras and when he had to step a little closer, and so on.

By Sunday, the crowd was smaller and he knew how to read it like they did. He hung back more, waited for their agreed-on signals.

The other bonus was that he got to spare more attention to watch River perform, and his heart lifted with excitement as the MC announced him.

He'd shed the naughty schoolgirl image of his first act and the nightie he'd finished the sexy near-striptease act in. For this, his third and final number, he was walking out in a gold-sequinned dress, already singing that classic about survival.

And... shit. His voice was resonant, even without the sound system. He was in four-inch heels, his lipstick shimmering with gold crystals.

It was hard to picture him being afraid and petrified, as the lyrics went, at all. Not like this.

He glowed with vitality, drinking in every focused gaze and reflecting that energy back on the crowd. Walking among the crowd, he deftly avoided one attempt to grab him —Zeph bristled and nearly started forward, but he didn't give the signal—and winked instead, indicating that tips could go into his bra.

Zeph watched in awe as River managed to turn the moment into that, then grabbed the guy's hand and let him get an extra squeeze of a tit.

When River was done with someone, he was done. He snapped away, gone before anyone got a second look at him. He was cruising the crowd for someone else to interact with. He found a college-aged girl and pulled her up to her feet, lifted her chin, encouraging her nonverbally to confidently lean in and sing the chorus.

By the time she sat, she glowed with a little extra confidence boost she hadn't had a moment ago.

River was *great* with people. He put himself down sometimes, but Zeph wished he had an ounce of the sparkle River did, no matter who he was around.

And he was beautiful, however the fuck he was dressed. His cheekbones were sharp, his lips full, his aura taking everything physical about him and projecting it twenty feet around him.

River was breathtaking.

Zeph realized his mouth was open and quickly cleared his throat as the song drew to a close, watching to make sure nobody had the wrong idea about whose turn it was to sing next.

The transition went seamlessly, and after a few more acts —lots more tips, a warm crowd tonight—it was over, everyone was bowing, blowing kisses, and the DJ took over to get the crowd dancing.

Zeph followed the last of the queens back to the dressing room, glancing around to make sure no strays snuck in.

By the time he reached the dressing room, it was *alive* with every ounce of glitz and energy he'd felt out there. It was just like his own locker room after a good fight night, coaches reliving the best moments with their guys, taping them up and checking them over, sometimes ribbing each other good-naturedly.

We're not so different, all of us.

River was in the center of it all, helping everyone get started undressing, and it took him a minute before he got his turn in front of the mirror in the staff room bathroom.

Zeph waited until he was alone in this moment to approach and congratulate him on the great show.

"Fucking thing," River was muttering as he tried to twist his hand behind himself to grab the zip. "Can anyone—" He spotted Zeph in the mirror and grinned. "My hero."

"Careful. My ego will swell." Zeph stepped behind him, a hand on his shoulder.

"And perhaps other things," River winked.

Zeph's cheeks flushed. He tried not to acknowledge it, tried not to let his body go there. Everyone was running on a post-show adrenaline high. He knew exactly what it was like. You were liable to talk to, kiss, fuck people you wouldn't otherwise just because your body needed the contact.

"Need a hand with that?"

They were inches apart—mostly vertically, with River still in those heels. Zeph could still easily see over River's shoulder, though, and the view of him in the mirror was a good one. Part of him itched to slide his arms around River's waist and hug him, but he resisted. Way personal contact for just-made-friends-again.

Those gold sequins on his lips looked scratchy, but there was gloss over them. Zeph found himself wondering what it would be like to kiss him again.

Up close, River looked like a fucking angel.

Get a grip, Zeph reminded himself sharply, but… the gold dust that shimmered over his cheeks, the platinum blond of his hair now that the wig was off, everything just seemed to glow with that spirit. Yellow, or gold, really was his color.

Only seconds had passed in his thorough scrutiny, but River hadn't missed the look over. "If you're offering." River's voice was quiet, but his gaze was still focused on Zeph's eyes. He hadn't looked away.

They were unnoticed in the midst of a few of the queens nearly screaming with laughter over one of them breaking a heel on the way into the dressing room, apparently.

This was a moment. Zeph could play along.

"I insist." Zeph felt the chemistry sizzle between them for a moment when his fingers touched the bare skin at the nape of River's neck. He tugged the zipper down the first few inches.

He instinctively shivered at the sound of metal catching metal on the way down. It was a primal, sexual noise, and his animal brain was kicking in. It was a fight to let go, but when the zipper dangled just under River's shoulder blades, he did.

And just in time.

"—who's car sharing? You two, are you?"

"Uh." Zeph's mind was on neither cars nor sharing, and Glam's question took him aback.

"We're carpooling," River answered, turning to reach behind himself and pull the zipper the rest of the way down.

Zeph slipped past Glam and out of the bathroom so he didn't see River half-naked. He watched the door and held accessories for a few of the queens, happy to be their coat rack while some of them got ready to leave the club and others got ready to party.

Zeph was sure as hell looking forward to the carpool tomorrow.

CHAPTER
Seven

RIVER

Perched on his hard-sided rolling suitcase, River tried not to shift his weight too much. He'd already once nearly rolled down the gently sloping sidewalk in front of his apartment building into the storm drain. His gym bag with his costumes and drag kit sat by his side.

All he was missing was his ride.

Taking one car with Zeph to Vegas sounded fantastic, yet terrifying. They weren't even driving in convoy to Vegas, so it was really just the two of them. And being alone with his ex for four hours? That was a recipe for disaster. Zeph was the only ex River would have said yes to, and even now, he was reconsidering that idea.

River had his ankle crossed over his knee, and he couldn't stop nervously jiggling his foot.

They'd been getting along fine—more than fine, if last night was any indication—at the club, but this was different.

He tried to look on the bright side: it was a chance to catch up on life.

Then, he worried again. What was he going to tell him?

What the hell had he done in the last five years? He hadn't gone back to school, hadn't discovered the cure for cancer, hadn't made the newspaper for anything. Jesus, was he going to come off as a total loser?

River nearly sprang to his feet when an engine purred nearby, smoothing his skirt down. It was going to be a hot drive, so he'd gone with a skirt and thigh-high stockings, and a flowery men's tank top—the obnoxious kind that showed off his nipples from the side. He'd be glad to get into the shade of the car, at least.

It had been a while since he'd been hiking outdoors, which he normally loved. All kinds of outdoorsy things, really, but he just hadn't made time lately. His heat tolerance had clearly suffered for it.

Zeph's car was a beaten-up old black thing, but it still sounded like it ran fine, which was all River cared about. He half-considered proposing they switch cars to his own pride and joy, and the result of several years of private makeup lessons—his little red Mazda—but he didn't want to sting Zeph's pride. Besides, he didn't want to test out Vegas car thieves.

"Well, hello." Zeph unbuckled and pushed open the door, then stepped out of the driver's seat. He reached for the gym bag.

River grinned. "Hey. Are you seriously taking my luggage?"

Zeph's eyes widened. He paused and blushed, the bag by his side. He slowly lowered it to the pavement. "No...?"

"Aw. My knight in..." River eyed the car. "Is that a very dark blue or black?"

"Blue." Zeph rolled his eyes when he realized River was

teasing and tossed the bag in the back seat before River hefted his suitcase in after it.

"In blue armor," River finished, closing the door and striding around to the passenger side.

"And my maiden in, uh. Whatever you call that," Zeph gestured down at River in a broad circle, then slid into the driver's seat.

River buckled up and shut his door, then smirked. "Legs."

"Smartass."

"You know it." The car was cool, but not ice cold. River had chosen his outfit well. "I figured the drive would be hot if we get in the sun."

"Yeah, no, smart." Zeph was in a t-shirt and jeans—again. Did the man wear anything else?

Yes, his brain supplied and reminded him of the visual of him in his training shorts, shirtless and sweaty.

As they pulled out onto the road, it occurred to River that Zeph didn't seem even a little nervous to see him. Zeph even made small talk about traffic and the cost of gas, and River's heart sank.

Their last meeting, at the show, there had been something there. A moment between them. He'd seen it—Zeph's fingers on his zipper, his gaze flickering down to his lips like he wanted to taste them.

And yeah, River had a strict *no exes* policy, but... five years ago? For a week and a half? Zeph barely counted as an ex. If they hadn't been goddamn interrupted, River would have gone for it.

He waited to see if Zeph would mention it, but by the time they were out of the goddamn snarl of L.A. traffic and on the 15 eastbound, Zeph still hadn't brought up that moment.

Why was he disappointed? This ought to make it easier to avoid fucking the guy when it was supposed to be strictly professional. Well, mostly professional. Flirting didn't count. And yeah, he *could* try mentioning it himself, but that was beside the point. He wanted Zeph to acknowledge it if he felt it, too.

It didn't take long before his brain-mouth filter failed him, though. They weren't even halfway through the drive before the hookup stories started. And even when they tried to change subjects, sex seemed to creep into the conversation.

Maybe it was River's fault, but he'd happily accept that blame.

"Which baseball team did you say came to train? Oh my God, I think I blew one of them. Well, two. At once. That was a *great* night. All my bases were loaded..."

Zeph laughed richly. "Still a sucker for an athlete, huh?"

"Oh, I'm not picky, but I do have a... special fondness for you guys. You keep your bodies in such good shape... and you know how to use your hips for maximum drive..." River knew he was crossing the line from the kind of dirty talk friends did to the kind you said when you wanted to get a guy in bed, but... fuck it.

Flirting hard was his special talent, and the scenery was boring.

Well, only one of those excuses was true.

"We do." Zeph glanced sideways at River. "Have you had a lot of serious boyfriends in the last... five years now, I guess?"

River hesitated, then smirked. "Seriously good in bed, yeah. Not, like, *I wanna marry him and have his babies*, though. Still playing both ends of the spectrum, being the usual...

freak. That's still hard for guys to deal with. They want a pretty face to fuck and ignore when he talks about nail polish, *or* a big rough dude to kayak with. Not both in a dress. You?"

"Nah."

"So, among the muscles you've been training…" River trailed off, his arm propped between them.

Zeph laughed and nodded. "Guilty. It sounds like we could give each other a run for our money."

"Wouldn't be the first time," River teased.

Scarlet was creeping up Zeph's cheeks. "I don't remember there being a lot of running."

"Or chasing. I was easy. *Was*," River snorted, revising his word choice. "*Am*."

Zeph raised a brow, and his voice was maybe half an octave lower—definitely a little more rumbly. "How easy?"

River loved hearing the effect he had on a guy when he was flirting. The sparks between them weren't just idly glancing off one another. They were feeling each other out, fueling whatever the hell was starting up again.

It wasn't just tension, though. It was *fun*, swapping stories and hearing about Zeph's favorite moments—the highlight had been a locker room story River could only imagine. And would, for a long time to come. Picturing Zeph naked in the locker room was enough to do things to him.

"Well, if the *I sucked off two baseball players at once because I couldn't decide which one to hit on* story wasn't a clue…" River winked.

This was the most fun he'd had in ages, including being on stage.

Zeph's laugh was a deep rumble. "You're still into a little more than missionary with the lights off, then, huh?"

"Of *course*," River gasped. "Who the fuck likes that? I mean, love-making now and then, if I were in love..." He waved a hand. That was a huge hypothetical, and one he never saw coming true. Not right now, anyway. "But that wouldn't be under the covers. Or with the lights off. Or probably missionary."

"So, no," Zeph laughed.

They'd fucked probably a dozen times in the lead-up to their relationship, plus the short-lived fling itself. The details were a little fuzzy, but on the whole, River was pretty sure none of them fit that description, either.

He *vividly* remembered fucking in the backroom of the club, his legs around Zeph's waist, tucked into the dark corner where they could barely even see each other, but catching just a glint of light on those dark, intense eyes locking with his as Zeph crushed him against the wall, kissed him like he was scarce oxygen for Zeph's soul...

The heat, the weight, the *size* of him. Oh, yeah, River remembered it well.

Not just because they'd gone out for pizza afterward and Zeph had admitted he'd just accepted the offer to train out in the midwest.

"You should show me what *you're* into these days." The dare slipped from his lips before he could even think twice about it.

Fuck. He'd laid it all bare, and they still had an hour in the car.

But Zeph was still smirking, casting sideways glances at him while watching the road. "I was waiting for you to ask. I thought we were one-and-done back then."

"Why?" River challenged, ignoring the small voice in the back of his head that reminded him, *Because that's been your policy since your first terrible-sex-with-ex lesson ten years ago, dumbass.*

Zeph moved his hand to River's knee, the weight of it solid and warm against him. "Good question."

"Seems like a dumb rule," River murmured, suddenly breathless. He squirmed in his seat, opening his legs a little wider as Zeph's fingers slowly trailed from his knee to the top of his stocking. "I don't like rules."

"I like this River." Zeph's fingers slipped into the hem of his stocking, running along it until he reached River's inner thigh.

"And this River would *love* a hand right now," River informed him as his cock throbbed with need against his underwear. Skintight boxer briefs didn't leave a lot of room for growth.

Zeph smirked playfully. "What do I get out of the deal? Other than a dry-cleaning bill for the upholstery?"

That made River snort with laughter. He cast a quick glance down at the bulge in Zeph's pants, then at the road ahead. It was a good, long straight stretch without many cars around. "How steady is your driving?"

"Really?" Zeph laughed, but there was a growl in the back of his throat, too. "Straight as an arrow."

"Still straight as can be with a cute little fag's mouth on your dick?" River breathed, unbuckling and scooting back in his seat. He hoisted up one knee against the seat, the other elbow resting on the center console between them as he swiveled.

"That..." Zeph's voice was strained. He shifted, pushing back in his seat and sitting as straight as he could to give River room between his crotch and the wheel. "That's very gay."

"Welcome to my world, baby." River pulled Zeph's zipper down, rubbing the bulge with his palm as he shoved his head under Zeph's arm. It was confined, but nothing he couldn't work with.

And Zeph was already breathing harshly, pushing his hips up into River's touch. "Fuck. Oh, my God, I can't believe you're that ballsy."

"A skirt can hide a lot."

"Oh, it does." While River hauled Zeph's jeans down, Zeph shifted his grip. One hand was still on the wheel, but the other ran over his head, then down his back. He cupped River's ass and squeezed, then walked his fingers up the bare thigh toward his ass.

"Oh, Jesus, you'll make me come on your seat if you finger me while I do this," River warned.

"Noted." Zeph pulled back and trailed his fingers along the backs of River's thighs. Zeph's cock was free—throbbing, swollen, big. Even bigger than he remembered. River wanted it sliding down his throat, *now*.

River moaned. "You better tell me you get your ass tested," he threatened. "Because I need my road trip protein."

"I do, thank God," Zeph breathily laughed. He ran his hand back up River's back, pushing his skirt up before running his hand to the back of River's head. He threaded his fingers through the longer hair at the top of his head. "Negative. Two weeks ago. Nobody since."

"Thank *fuck*. That's the other thing about athletes," River whispered, licking the swollen head. "You look after yourselves."

A choked moan was Zeph's only response. Muscles in his hips twitched and his hand pushed on River's head for a moment before he relaxed his arm. He was clearly trying not to push himself up into River's mouth. He slid his hand down to River's back instead.

River sucked in his cheeks and twirled his tongue around the head a few times, lapping it slowly before he pulled his mouth off and kissed his way down the shaft.

He mouthed at it, open-mouthed kisses all the way down to Zeph's balls, then back up.

"Fucking tease," Zeph growled. "I remember that."

River smirked. "Do you?" He ran his hand down the shaft to grip it at the base so he could press his lips hard against the tip, slowly sliding it between his pursed lips. He was thick and hot, veiny on his tongue.

Zeph's only answer was a grunt of need. "Cocktease. Still."

River drew his mouth up and off with a quiet pop, then licked the tip again for good measure. "You make it fun. Still."

"Fuck off."

"Gladly." River started to shift as if to squirm back toward his own seat, but Zeph grabbed him by the hair. Exactly what he wanted.

"Smartass."

River twisted to glance over his shoulder. The awkward crouch sure pushed him up into the air, doggy-style. "It looks *very* smart in this skirt."

"Jesus!" Zeph growled, but he didn't shove River's head down. The muscles in his arms were rippling, though.

River laughed richly and relented, sucking that thick cock into his mouth again to bob his head hard and fast. Going at it sideways was a little different, but nothing he hadn't done before.

Not with Zeph, though.

"Yes… yeah! River," Zeph moaned, keeping his other hand

white-knuckle tight on the wheel. "Fuck, yeah. Oh, Jesus. You're still the best I ever... *fuck*, I'm gonna come so fast. That thing... with your tongue..."

Best of any guy? Really? River stifled his amusement and made a mental note to ask later.

Zeph's hand sliding off his head to the wheel was endlessly satisfying, even if it sent a hard rush of adrenaline pounding through his body.

Yeah, road head was a stupid idea, but enough people did it that it had its own name. And he could see the appeal. The danger, the exhibitionist thrill, the spontaneity...

The salty taste of liquid hitting the back of his throat as Zeph shouted in pleasure, his hips pushing forward—hard— into River's mouth. River swallowed hard, his mouth filling with Zeph's passion between each gulp, lips pursing around twitching skin, nose buried in his shirt.

When Zeph caught his breath, vocalizing his breathing as he panted and pulled himself together, River pulled his head up slowly, starting to squirm backward.

"Oh, no, you don't." Zeph pulled his head down onto his lap, then ran his hand down River's chest as River awkwardly turned onto his side, then his back. The steering wheel with one strong forearm blocking his view of the car roof, and Zeph's flushed, intense face... that was all he could see.

River's heart raced. His boner was pushing up his skirt, he was so in need of Zeph's attention. "Can you reach?"

"I nearly fingered that hot little ass a minute ago," Zeph pointed out. "So... probably." Zeph's hand was at his waistband, playing with it.

"Can you reach *and* stay on the road?"

"We'll find out, won't we?" Zeph's cocky grin should have

worried him, or irritated the shit out of him, but River couldn't help a grin back at him.

"Jesus. If you kill us, I'ma haunt your ass, bitch," River informed him. "And not like Ghost. Paranormal Witness. Paranormal *Survivor*." But Zeph's hand was pushing his skirt up, sliding into his tight boxer-briefs, and he couldn't think straight anymore. "Hnnh!"

"That shut you up," Zeph observed mildly, but his touch was far from mild. Slow, so fucking slow and deliberate, *strong*. Fingers curled around his shaft, working it gently free from his underwear and the skirt to the open air of the car.

At least in the right-hand lane, nobody would pass them on his side and straight up get *that* view. "A dick in my mouth does the same," River retorted. He twisted to kiss the tip of Zeph's soft manhood open-mouthed.

"Careful. We've still got a couple hours. I might just keep you here." Zeph's voice was a low growl.

That idea sounded a hell of a lot more tempting than he'd probably meant it to. Or maybe he *had* meant it to sound like River's idea of a perfect afternoon.

He couldn't help his shiver, thrusting up into Zeph's tight grip as he dug his heel into the back of the seat and twisted himself to try to get his leg anywhere other than dangling out the window.

"Jesus. You nearly came on the spot. Still a kinky bastard, aren't you?" Zeph's grip was still tight, but he was only stroking slowly.

River groaned. "If this is payback for teasing you, I'm sorry."

"No, you're not." Zeph's eyes sparkled as he risked a glance down from the road to River's face. "Liar."

Busted. He loved drawing it out, making men—not just

any man, making *Zeph*—big, strong, tough fighter Zeph—making *him* need him so badly he was reduced to begging.

River just closed his eyes and moaned, rolling his head back in Zeph's lap. Those strong thighs were probably the most comfortable part of him, between the foot jammed between the car door and seat, his other leg splayed out toward the dash, the gear shift pressing into his back.

But Zeph's strokes sped up, tightened around him, squeezing him onward as electric need crackled under his skin.

He was quivering now, ecstasy building under his skin with every confident, self-assured upward jerk or downward press of Zeph's hand.

River pressed the back of his head harder into Zeph's leg, his gaze focusing on the strong forearm still gripping the wheel.

He's got me.

He let go.

River couldn't remember the last time he came so hard. The cry that ripped from the back of his throat left him hoarse, instantly struggling not to cough on the dry desert air, but his muscles were too fucking busy doing *this*.

His body rippled and pushed up in a wave, rising up and stiffening as his hips subconsciously pushed up into Zeph's hand until he practically sprawled on the dash. Anyone in the oncoming lane could get an eyeful of his half-naked body and the last shudders of pleasure, and the goddamn mess he left on his clothes.

Fucking finally, he collapsed on the seat again, another wrung-out cry slipping from his lips. "Zeph. Fuck."

"Jesus *fuck*, River!" River peeked through his lashes to interpret the tone. Zeph's cheeks were blazing red. He was slack-jawed, and he kept sneaking glances down at River's face, then over the length of his body.

River managed a cheeky smile. "You stayed on the road."

"Oh, you're fucking gorgeous when you come. If we weren't in this car…" There was a promise in Zeph's voice.

Like that, he'd caught River's interest. "What would you have done?"

"Spoilers, sweetheart."

River twisted for a better look up the length of Zeph's body, from his magnificent cock against his thigh to the t-shirt that clung to his rippling pecs. "It's only a spoiler if you plan to follow through."

Zeph hesitated, rubbing his hand along River's thigh and then slowly up his side until he cupped his cheek. "Are we…?"

Jesus, the gear shift in his back was going to fuck his posture if he didn't sit up now. River twisted and did just so, pulling away to sit upright. His mind worked through Zeph's half-formed question.

Dating again? Hell, no. Not a second time. That went against his rules. And not so fast. But it would be a sin to pass up more sex with this gorgeous creature.

"What happens in Vegas," River succinctly told Zeph. "How about we hook up for the tour? It's ten more days."

"Ten *more* days, you mean." Zeph's lips twitched into a smile as he referenced their attempt at a relationship.

"Exactly. Ten days to get it out of our system. No strings attached."

It was a casual proposition, but River's heart thudded as he gazed sideways at Zeph, holding his breath.

Come on, baby. Say yes to me one more time.

"FINE. SO WE MAY HAVE AN AGREEMENT. FOR THE DURATION of our Vegas tour."

"*Aha!*" RB was grinning at him, entirely too triumphantly. "I saw him getting handsy when he helped you unload. Heh, so to speak."

For half a second, River had the wild idea RB meant… but no, RB would have honked. Still, it left him off-kilter just enough to say more than he might have.

And RB had just winked. "You tell him you need extra help guarding your body? Nice excuse."

River couldn't help himself. "It's not like *that*."

RB cast him a scrutinizing look. "This isn't just a Vegas fling?"

By all accounts, River should have said *no, that's all it is*. Because that *was* all it was. But instead, he shot the rest of his whisky, then put his foot in his mouth. "You know *the one that got away*? He's the closest thing I've got to one of those."

RB looked stunned. He turned on his bar stool to face River. "You never told us *that*."

"It's not exactly relevant," River muttered, but he knew it was an excuse. He looked around the little dive bar. It was just around the corner from the motel where they were staying—just off the Strip, and pretty damn cheap.

"I saw the way you were looking at him in our L.A. shows, too. And earlier, before we all split up to explore for tonight."

River's cheeks flushed. He signalled the bartender for two more, not looking in RB's eye.

RB whistled under his breath. "You look a little invested for a short-term thing."

"Nah." River shrugged it off, trying to play it as casual as he could. He might have told RB more, but they were in public, and even in Vegas, he felt like even existing in a smoky straight dive bar was pushing it. "Not here."

Should've shaved better. Or put on full foundation to cover the stubble. He'd gone with a collared shirt and jeans, but with his hair and makeup, he wasn't exactly the most intimidating.

Right on cue, his heart sank. He saw RB's reaction to the presence behind him and felt him before he heard the words. "Don't want us overhearing your homo love life woes?" The words were drawled out like the guy barely knew what the last word meant.

River turned on his stool to take in the guy, who looked exactly how he'd pictured half a second ago: beefy, close-cropped hair, a couple of arm tattoos, and a sneer on his face as he looked at River.

River knew the look well: the disgust that curled their lips was impossible to mask. Even people who could handle him making out with a guy in front of them would suddenly react like he'd erupted three pounds of live spiders from his chest, Alien-style, at the sight of a little lip gloss.

He couldn't even tell if the guy was a straight jackass or one of those too-masc-for-you dudes who bashed fags in the front room and fucked them in the back.

"Why? You offering to be my *homo* agony aunt?" River drew himself slightly forward, shifting his weight in case he needed to slide off in a hurry and duck—or hit. "Or did you just remember what century we're living in?"

The guy sneered back at him. "Fuck, no. Keep it to yourself."

"Really?" River eased to his feet. "Why don't you ask everyone around us if we were disturbing all of them with our *faggotry*? Or no, because *you're* the only creepy mother-fucker listening in on everyone's conversations. Shoo," he flapped a hand toward the other side of the bar.

The guy was staring back at him, mouth a little open, eyes glazed over. He was looking at River the way River imagined he'd look at a bit of food that refused to come unstuck from his shirt.

Looking River up and down, he licked his lips.

A particularly tasty morsel, River amended that thought with an inward shudder. These were the creepiest assholes of all, literally ignoring his objections in favor of whatever fucked-up fantasies they had playing in their heads about men in skirts. Thank God Zeph wasn't that kind of guy.

River started to take a step forward, but he felt RB's hand on his shoulder blade, reminding him gently that they were in a public bar where they had every right to be. And it wasn't a backwater town in Tennessee. No need to escalate.

So River flapped a hand, again, this time making a bigger motion of it to catch the bartender's eye. "I said, *shoo*."

With that, the guy turned and left—not just for the other side of the bar, but out of it altogether.

"Jesus," River muttered, sinking onto his stool again. He hadn't even gotten to rip into the guy properly before RB had reminded him that he didn't want to spend an hour every day covering the black eye.

RB pushed his whisky toward him. "Why don't you tell me about the two of you?"

"Nothing to tell." He didn't relish the thought of talking about his homo love life in front of everyone here—nobody had jumped in to second the guy, but nobody had stood up for him, either.

"Mmm." RB's eyes narrowed, and then he shot his whisky. "Come on. Let's find a liquor store and my room."

There was an idea he could get on board with.

CHAPTER
Nine

ZEPH

IT WAS A PRETTY GENERIC MOTEL ROOM OFF THE STRIP—although Zeph hadn't stayed in Sin City for a couple of years, it was exactly as seedy as he remembered.

No way was he hanging around this dump when he could be at a gym.

Zeph cast his mind over his phone contacts. Who was likely to be in town and want to meet up? He considered a group text, but he didn't want to be That Guy rolling into town, expecting the red carpet unrolled in front of him.

His gaze landed on one name: Rhino.

Yeah, Rhino was a good guy, and he trained here in one of the rural counties with legal brothels by the fake ranches for tourists. The two of them had fought a few times, and they'd trained together when Rhino visited Chicago.

More importantly, they could watch tonight's fight together and get a sense for each other's reactions, ahead of his fight with Rhino not even two months from now. Wouldn't hurt to get on better terms and pick up a few hints while letting him see a few tricks, too.

Zeph typed a quick text.

You in Vegas? Here for a week.

The response was quick.

Hey! Yeah come watch fight night. 1385 W Chestnut.

Score. Zeph changed into his fighting trousers and a light t-shirt, casting a quick glance at the door.

Right. He was sharing. He'd have to get used to sharing space with someone. He didn't even share a room with his trainer, Bo. They'd tried and nearly killed each other a few years back at 2am over B-list movies.

When Zeph stepped into the gym, a shiver ran down his spine. On instinct, he straightened up, walking like one of the pros, not the audience who shuffled in with their beer and popcorn, breaths bated, eyes fixed on the cage.

God, he loved the sport. Not just his own fights, but the atmosphere in here that was so thick you could taste it. The excitement. The respect between the guys who were getting ready to beat each other up in a hopefully fair, clean fight.

Sometimes it was neither, but there was no fake shit going on at their level. Audiences didn't want that, fighters didn't want that… nobody did.

Zeph's mind was still half on River, who'd be waiting for him back at the motel by the time he got back. He'd said he wouldn't have a late night, and the fight probably wouldn't run that long either.

That thought didn't dispel the excitement thrumming under his skin, like something of its own that sparked to life every time they touched.

There was Rhino, in the front seats, an arm stretched casually over an empty seat next to him, presumably keeping it for him. Zeph grinned and headed down to join him, walking quietly over the boards until he flung himself into the seat.

He made Rhino jump, then smack the back of his chair.

"Asshole," Rhino greeted.

Zeph grinned at him and clapped his hand, pulling him in for a half-hug, half-back pat. "As always."

"How you been, man? Been forever since I was up in Chi-town."

"You won't find me there no more," Zeph countered. "I'm out in L.A. these days."

"No shit! Living?"

"Trying," Zeph laughed. SoCal cost of living was brutal. He couldn't do it if it weren't for the cheap apartment he'd found not far from his gym, in a pretty industrial part of town. Hell, if he lost the next couple fights, he wouldn't be able to keep doing it.

But there, he had a better chance of getting spotted by a gym owner who needed the equivalent of mid-list talent, sort of like his friend Tris. Thinking about his career sucked, so he stopped.

"First one... who's your money on?"

"Hayden. No doubt." Hayden was from Rhino's gym, so he'd expected the answer, but Rhino sounded like he meant it.

"Really?"

"Oh, yeah. Man, you should see how hard he's been train-ing. BJJ every day, too. And he's gone some kind of plant-powered raw vegan, eating pounds of bananas or something."

Huh. Not to be underestimated, then. Zeph had learned that the hard way: the young ones might not have experience in the cage, but they sure as hell had the endurance to train 24/7, even when they weren't getting ready for a fight. Brazilian Jiu Jitsu was a good style for him, from what Zeph knew about him.

"Jesus. It's all I can do not to inhale In'n'Out and a six-pack."

The first fight was fast and clean. Like Rhino had predicted, Hayden won, and he did have some explosive moves Zeph hadn't seen from him before. They were both new, essentially opening for the fight everyone was waiting for.

Tex and Danny were both big names—bigger than even Rhino and Zeph. By the time Zeph checked over his shoulder again, he found the seats filled.

"Jesus, they pulled a big crowd."

"You ever seen them live?" Zeph shook his head, and Rhino raised his brows. "Really?"

"Just never made it to the right place at the right time. Why?"

"They both have that kind of…"

"Zing." Zeph nodded. There was something electric about watching certain fighters live that TV could never capture.

The charge in the air, the taste of victory, the inevitable rebound from the underdog, the give-and-take until they both decided they were going for the win… but that was common to every fight.

Some guys had something more—the magnetism like glue, keeping the audience focused on them against all the odds. Rhino had it. He was smart, cagey, aggressive in the corner but playful in the middle of the ring. Zeph hoped he did, too.

Just as Rhino predicted, Zeph found himself sucked into the fight the moment it began. His eyes flickered between them both, trying to measure them up as they sized each other up.

Rhino leaned in and murmured, "You hear Midtown's folding?"

"Isn't that—"

"Where Danny trains." Rhino nodded. "Uh huh."

"Where's he going?"

"Depends how he does today."

Zeph winced. If he felt desperate, this could turn ugly fast. He kept his fingers crossed that Danny remembered how good he was—how easily he'd get sponsorship some-where else. He racked his brain for their records lately. He'd missed Danny's last fight, but Tex had to have won three, four in a row now?

"That's new," he murmured when Tex started with a few short, sharp jabs toward Danny's solar plexus. Normally he went a little higher, trying to knock the opponent off-balance.

Danny easily avoided and countered with a leg sweep, but Tex side-stepped it as they circled.

The fighters were getting the crowd warmed up while testing each other. Both of them recognized it, and they swapped smiles as the two traded easy blows to dodge before closing in on each other.

"You hear Danny lost by TKO last fight?" Rhino murmured.

He winced. "No. Didn't the fight before...?"

"Yeah, he's had two in a row now. This could be the third. But last time was really a KO. Got listed as TKO."

"Fuck." A chill went down Zeph's spine as he watched them trading real blows now, the thudding of gloves on bodies sending a bloodthirsty cheer through the crowd. "He looked conscious?"

"Yeah. He told me later it was worse than it looked."

"He hasn't gotten a medical suspension yet?"

"No, but if he—ouch," Rhino hissed as Danny took a blow to the chin and stumbled to the mat. "If he gets KO'd today…"

He better get out while he still has a good head on his shoulders. Zeph winced, trying not to think about his own record this year. He was only in three fights this year, and he'd won two, but the third had nearly put him out of commission all summer.

Talking shop while sweat and blood tinged the air was nothing new to them, but it kept his mind off the upcoming fight they had together.

It was no surprise when the referee called it against Danny. The crowd went wild, but Rhino and Zeph stayed seated, applauding Tex's win.

It had been clean, all things considered. Would have been cleaner if Danny hadn't tried a desperate rush at the last minute, when he knew he was going to lose.

With the adrenaline still pumping, Zeph clapped Rhino's shoulder and hugged him tightly goodbye before slipping out the gym door, hoping to beat the crowds through the parking lot. Last thing he wanted was to be recognized and stopped for autographs or something.

Zeph was more on edge on his way out than when he'd walked in. All the way back to the motel, he replayed the critical moments in his head, and Rhino's hints.

BJJ… was Rhino taking up Brazilian Jiu Jitsu, too? Or was that a red herring? That would be a total departure from his usual training routine, but it was worth mentioning to Bo.

See if Bo could dig up anything on Rhino's routine leading up to their fight.

That was the problem with going to others' fights—by the time Zeph left, he was aching to be in the cage himself.

He had a lot on his mind he needed to sweat out.

CHAPTER

Ten

RIVER

APPARENTLY, ONE DRINK WAS ALL IT TOOK TO MAKE RIVER spill the beans on Zeph.

It was just as well, though. He never performed well on a hangover, and their first show was tomorrow. Still, RB had teased him about how fast he'd told him most of the details of their prior relationship.

Whatever. River was basically an open book about everyone and everything. He wasn't going to start keeping secrets now, because of this one guy.

While he waited for Zeph to get back from whatever gym he'd vaguely mentioned before they split, he tried to find something good on TV. Flicking through all the channels twice didn't turn up anything except The Wizard of Oz.

That was appropriate.

River smirked and left it on, checking his emails. Unsurprisingly, he had something waiting from one of the new queens. Anna Naz was the last queen driving into town tonight, and she was nervous as hell about her first show on the road. Poor thing.

He sent off a quick email in response, reminding her that Vegas was going to be a blast and she couldn't back out now anyway, she'd be leaving Tina without a roommate and *someone* needed to look after her.

There—a car engine. Right outside the motel room window.

River's breath caught, but he tried to be cool. He was still sprawled on the bed as he closed his laptop and put it aside, then finger-combed his hair into place, laced his fingers behind his head, fluffed the pillows behind him, and turned his gaze to the TV.

The knob rattled and then… God, Zeph looked good framed by a door.

"Hey," River greeted as if he hadn't been expecting him.

Zeph grunted and nodded, letting the door swing shut as he kicked off his shoes. "Had a good night?"

"Yeah. You?"

"Yep," Zeph confirmed.

"How'd the fights go?"

"Good." Zeph's gaze swept the room, from his bed to the TV, then River. He kept his eyes fixed on River as he steered around the end of his bed to sit on River's.

His brain was clearly not in conversation mode. River loved it when Zeph was clinging to the edge of decency, trying to contain that raw *need* that could make him throw River into bed from halfway across the room. Maybe he should get up and make him do it.

"Blocking my view there," River teased, turning down the volume as the bed sank under Zeph's weight.

Zeph glanced briefly at the TV again, then smirked as he looked back. "You a friend of Dorothy?"

"I know her well. A little birdie told me you do, too." River wagged a finger at him.

Zeph's eyes crinkled in that sweet, rare smile. "We have that in common." His eyes darkened again, swept down River's body from head to toe. It was all River could do not to moan when Zeph turned toward him and rested a hand on his knee. "What did you have to drink?"

"Not nearly enough to worry, baby," River whispered, his voice coming out more soft and hoarse than he'd meant it to.

Zeph turned away from the TV to face him, then crawled up the bed, pushing his knees apart.

Oh, God, River had missed having his weight between his legs, the heat radiating from his body between their chests as Zeph pressed himself carefully against River, as if afraid he would break him…

"Get down here," River growled, grabbing Zeph by the shoulders to haul him down. He ground against the firm weight on him, running his hands up Zeph's back under his t-shirt and pressing his lips into the crook of Zeph's neck.

"I've been waiting for this," Zeph breathed out, his own breath hot against River's ear. He licked slowly around the rim until River's knees went weak, then pressed his hardening cock into River's thigh when he spread his legs further, letting Zeph even closer.

They were way overdressed. Luckily, it seemed Zeph agreed. He pulled back to start hauling clothes off both of their bodies in no particular order. As he pushed River's shirt off, Zeph's palm brushed River's bare chest for the first time in years, sending electric sparks of desire jolting through his bones.

"Fuck." River's head rolled back into the pillow as he squeezed his eyes shut, raising his arms obediently.

Zeph slowed for a moment, brushing his fingertips across River's nipple, then yanked his shirt off.

"Nnh. Please. *Please*," River breathed out, not even sure what he was begging for. He was already naked otherwise, and the scrape of fabric against his legs told him that Zeph had another couple layers to go.

River shivered as Zeph groaned in appreciation for his neediness, then whispered, "Hold on, baby."

Within moments, Zeph was naked, skin on hot skin. River was already burning up, pressing every inch of himself into Zeph and wrapping his legs tightly around Zeph's waist.

"You make it so damn easy," Zeph growled. "I love it."

River pressed his lips against Zeph's throat. "The better to fuck me."

"Oh, I'm about to."

Zeph's hand ran slowly, deliberately, from his hip, a finger tracing over his hipbone until he shuddered, then up his side. By the time Zeph got to his ribs, River was biting back his needy noises.

Zeph ran his finger along the edge of his armpit, skimming the muscle by his shoulder blade, and River's nipples were impossibly hard, his dick twitching against Zeph's thigh as the muscles in his body all clenched and shuddered. Zeph pulled his hand up to lick his own palm.

"You fucking *tease*." River loved it, though. Not many guys took the time to slow down, even when it was clearly about to get fast and hard, and make him *ache* for it.

Jesus. They hadn't fucked in five years, but their sexual chemistry was as instant and explosive as if they'd never left the bed.

One of Zeph's hands slid between their bodies as he pulled his hips back a little to give himself room. River's whine of complaint was cut off when Zeph's strong, wet grip wrapped around their shafts and squeezed them together.

"Oh, fuck," was all he managed before Zeph thrust, spreading slickness along both their shafts. "Yes...!"

Zeph's lips were on his, exactly as hot and fierce as he needed them. Zeph's tongue forced its way between River's lips, his nose rubbed River's, his lips sucked River's lower lip into his mouth, and then he bit.

River held still, a faint but high-pitched sound of need falling from his mouth before Zeph pulled back from the kiss, leaving his lips almost sore, and slapped his hip.

"Turn over."

Oh, God, yes. River pulled his knees up to his chest to untangle his legs from Zeph's, then rolled, squeezing between Zeph's body and the bed and somehow managing to get onto his front.

Zeph's hardness pressed against the inside of his thigh, then bumped his balls, ground against his crack, and Zeph was squeezing his thighs together, thrusting between them a couple of times.

"*Fuck*," River whimpered. "Hurry up...!"

The tease of having that thick shaft against him, but not in him, was almost too much. He was empty, and he needed Zeph in him.

"Yes, sir. You pick up anyone else lately?"

River snorted as he grabbed a pillow to bury his face in when the going got good. "In the six hours since we got here?"

"You're the one who tried to blow the whole team," Zeph reminded him, and River could tell by his tone he was grinning.

"Fuck off," River laughed. "Use one anyway, asshole."

"Did I earn that?" Zeph clicked his tongue as he ripped open a condom. "Oops."

"You did. But I *am* a slut for a good cock," River agreed. When warm fingers pressed at his opening, then inside, he let out his breath and moaned. When he'd collected his wits enough again, he mumbled, "Or fingers, or toys, or..."

"One thing at a time," Zeph reminded him. "We've got over a week left."

River did some quick mental math. If he could get Zeph on his own a few times a day, that was... a whole lot of sex. Jesus, this trip was a good idea.

He started squirming, pushing up into Zeph's fingers as he tightened around them, gasping for breath into the fabric. Zeph was rubbing his prostate, maddeningly slow.

"*Fuck* the teasing," River finally hissed, and Zeph got the message. Fingers were replaced by a thick cock head pressing into him, filling him inch by inch with hard heat. Zeph's nails dug into his hip, keeping him in place.

"Fuck, you're good," Zeph breathed out, his teeth grazing the edge of River's jaw. He pulled back and nibbled behind his ear, then kissed the back of his neck.

River had lost the capacity for language, except, "Yes," and, "Fuck," and most of all, "Zeph!"

Zeph fucked him like a machine. Every thrust of his hips was smooth, but that didn't mean he couldn't pound him hard and fast, too. Jesus, River never wanted this moment to end.

A hand slipped under him, between the sheets and his chest, and then Zeph was tweaking his nipple.

River remembered one more word: "Christ!" He threw his head back, knocking it into Zeph's shoulder.

Zeph's rhythm stuttered for a moment before he picked up the pace again, hard and fast, grunting into his ear.

That sound—pure, animalistic need—was what flung River over the edge.

He came hard, desperate for a hand stroking him off but hands-free nonetheless, clenching around Zeph as Zeph slowed the pace for just a minute, letting him ride out every wave of pleasure that hit him.

Then, Zeph pinned him down by the shoulder and fucked him hard and fast. A few thrusts later, Zeph gasped. "Fuck… Yes! River!"

"Come for me, baby," River breathed out, his cheeks flushed and head spinning. Zeph used him the way he needed to, and River fucking loved every moment of it.

Zeph pounded into him hard as he came, one arm wrapped around his waist while the other hand still kept him pinned to the bed. When his thrusts finally slowed, his grip loosened, and he slumped on top of River for a few moments.

Damp skin on skin was almost unbearably hot with River's skin still burning, but he grinned to himself and let Zeph take a moment. Zeph's hand was on his side now, tracing his ribs and running down to caress his hip where his nails had dug in.

"Fuck. That might bruise."

"Good," River breathed out, twisting to check it. It was nowhere his costumes should reveal anyway.

Zeph chuckled deeply. "Kinky bastard."

"Just the way you like it." River felt empty as Zeph slid out and rolled off him, but Zeph's weight stayed right there by his side. A hand slid up to his chest to roll him over onto his side so Zeph could spoon him.

"Ooh," River breathed out. This way, he could see the TV, and Zeph could watch over his shoulder. "Mmm, we just got to the good part."

"I feel that way, too," Zeph murmured.

River cracked a grin. "So romantic," he teased.

"Never. I mean the bumsex."

"The—" River's laugh was quick and loud. It took a lot to take him by surprise, but Zeph had it mastered. "The bumsex?"

"The smoking *hot* anal, if you'd rather."

"Yeah, that," River giggled. "Oooh! Glinda's wand. You know, I always wanted one."

Zeph gave him a quick grope. "I think you were blessed with one."

"Hey!" River laughed, squirming with the overstimulation before Zeph let go. "So were you. Jesus."

"You all right? I didn't hurt you, did I?" Zeph murmured.

God, he was sweet. A ten-night-stand wasn't supposed to care about that. River twisted to give him a fond smile over his shoulder, then tilted his chin to indicate that Zeph should kiss him. When he did, River murmured, "I'm fine. I can play rough. You did pickup soccer with me that time, didn't you?"

"Mmm," Zeph hummed.

"And you know I like it when you pound me through the bed... or the wall..."

"Careful what you say. My wand's always listening."

River smirked. "I hope so. I can whisper a little closer to it if it needs it."

Zeph's breath caught in his throat for a distinct moment before he tickled River's ribs. "You're dirty."

"You are too, you filthy animal." River slapped away Zeph's hand. "We're missing the movie, shut up."

"You shut up," Zeph laughed.

Before River could think up a joke to crack about wanting Zeph to make him make more noise, his eyelids were too warm and heavy to think straight. He curled up against Zeph's chest to watch the old movie until he slept.

"Whoa. The fountains! Look-look-look, that's the one that puts on the show!"

Glam made a little tongue clicking noise at Anna. "Don't stare like a tourist."

"But we're tourists. We're supposed to stare at tourist attractions," she objected, pushing back her wig and strutting on with the group down the Strip, where Zeph was desperately trying to shepherd everyone to the right bar on time.

Tina piped up, "Darling, we *are* the tourist attractions."

She wasn't wrong. There were phones pointed toward them as they walked, a cacophony of high heel noises accompanying them, and every shutter click made Zeph twitch slightly.

He stayed calm and steady outwardly, keeping his eyes peeled every which way for signs of trouble, but nobody seemed to want to start anything. If anything, here, they were just an amusement.

River was passing out flyers to anyone who took a photo, sashaying from one side of the group to the other with ease, smiling and flirting and giggling like he was having the time of his life. Knowing him, he probably was.

"Darlings, it's Vegas. It's not going to go away. Keep your cool," Glam advised. She'd been there before, as had a few others, including Zeph, but not everyone.

Everyone else who was oohing and ahhing at every hotel on the Strip *was* drawing eyes, but Zeph had the feeling River wasn't discouraging them precisely so that they'd attract attention and he could hand out more show flyers. He'd already gone through half the stack.

By the time they got to the little bar where they were holding the show, every one of them was relieved to put down her bag and get to work dressing.

In the meantime, Zeph headed up to the bar with River to talk to management.

They exchanged formalities and chatted about their plans for the night while River handed over the music CD to give to the DJ. But it didn't take long before Sean, the night manager, turned his eye to Zeph.

"And are you in the show, too? As a prop?"

Zeph feigned offence. "I can dance quite well, if you give me a tune." River snorted with laughter and he shoved him slightly.

Sean giggled and scooted closer along the bar, then wrapped an arm around his bicep. "I imagine you have a hard time finding dresses that fit those guns."

Oh, boy. You could be a little more subtle. Zeph was fine with being hit on, but with River right there, he didn't think too closely about tugging River close to him. "If my b... if my boss would let me, I'd be in the show in a heartbeat."

"I'm only saving you from yourself," River giggled, not pulling back.

Zeph didn't want to think too much about why his first instinct had been to pull River close and say he was with him. *Boss* had not been the first word to his lips.

Actually, now that he thought about the day, he'd checked in more on River, he'd looked over his way more... he'd looked at him first for guidance. Which was normal, since River was technically the one who'd hired him, right?

River disappeared to get dressed, leaving him to make small talk with Sean for a few minutes. Luckily, Sean had likely sensed something between them, since he'd pulled back to mild flirtation.

By the time he made it back to the dressing room, the thrum of adrenaline was palpable. River was darting around doing his usual last-minute makeup fixes on everyone else, Glam was in charge of ensuring everyone made it to the stage with all their props, and Anna just seemed to be frozen on the spot watching everything unfold.

Before Zeph could make it over to her and attempt a pep talk, River spotted her, sidled up and hugged her, and murmured with her for a minute. Whatever he said got her smiling, then moving with them.

Zeph shook his head slightly as River passed, giving him an admiring glance, and River winked back at him.

Then they were up, Tina taking the stage to announce the first number of the night.

It was a different routine than L.A., since not everyone from those shows had been able to make it out here. Zeph wasn't yet sure when it was safe to get between their makeshift dressing room and the little stage at the back of the bar. In the end, he picked a spot near the side of the stage, just in the shadows but visible to anyone looking for security.

"And all the way from the frozen north of Minnesota, the lady of the hour escaped on a dogsled—seemingly forgetting all her clothes in the process, but we like her that way—to join us tonight!"

Half the audience groaned at the song choice as Let It Go began to play while River strutted out onto stage.

Despite the horrible music choice, River hammed it up and turned it into a sexy striptease number about letting go of his clothing, going all the way from a sweater to bikini top, and some kind of bulky skirt to a miniskirt in the process, and managing to make it look both sexy and sweet.

That was just River's charm. Sexy *and* sweet.

Zeph reminded himself to watch the audience, not the performance. Rule number one of security.

River's numbers were the most interesting to him throughout the rest of the show, too, but Zeph slowly relaxed throughout the course of the night. The crowd was very well-behaved—only at one point between numbers did he have to intervene when two drunk guys were arguing over whose turn it was to shove tips into Glam's bikini top.

They were about to start a fight over something... this was just an excuse, he could tell.

Zeph muscled in between and made them take turns being very well-behaved with him standing right there, which amused the people nearby. He made a mental note to refer the club's security to them, but when he made eye contact, the guy at the door nodded slightly. They were already on it.

God, it was nice working with professionals. For Vegas, the bar was tiny, but their people were well-trained.

The show ended without incident, though, and Zeph was

glad of it. He didn't want to take more bruises than he had to, even if he was prepared to do so.

"I'm glad you were on the ball there," River murmured afterward in the dressing room as he unzipped his bikini top.

Zeph's eyes fell to the mirror, watching his bare chest for a moment before he yanked his gaze north again. "Uh huh. That's my job."

"I like your whole muscled enforcer look. You should try it on me sometime," River teased, but only Zeph knew that was a much more immediate invitation.

He had to fight not to grin all the way back to their motel. God, this job was great. The pay was shit, but the rest of the benefits?

Out of this world.

CHAPTER

Twelve

RIVER

THE PILLOW WAS SOFT, THE BLANKETS WERE WARM, AND THE space heater of a firm, muscled body beside him was—for once—welcome.

River smiled before he even cracked his eyes, rubbing at his eyes for a moment. It took him a moment to realize who exactly he was in bed with. Then, his smile grew.

As he stretched, his mind cast back over last night. God, it had been a good night in every sense. From a nearly flawless opening night in Vegas to going home with Zeph, checking off a few more boxes on his to-do list…

And spending the night in Zeph's bed was always welcome. Zeph slept like a rock, and tolerated his touchy-feely sleeping habits.

It was a little embarrassing—no matter who he shared a bed with, River wound up wrapped around them with all his limbs by the end of the night. Because of it, and his reluctance to encourage romantic feelings toward every one-night-stand that happened into his life, he rarely *slept* with others.

But Zeph was different. They had an arrangement. So River was going to take full advantage while he could.

River's gaze wandered down those broad shoulders, the steady swell and dip of Zeph's ribs, the tattoo along his arm... He let himself perv on Zeph while deciding how pissed off his lover would be if he woke him for a round of morning sex.

Just when he'd decided to go for it, there was a soft knock on the door.

River heaved a slow sigh. Maybe someone had nerves, or wanted to go over last night's show, or needed help finding a good breakfast spot... somehow, he'd wound up taking partial charge of the group. They looked to him for guidance along with the official leaders, Tina and Glam, even though he was only supposed to be in charge of makeup.

River pulled on sweatpants on the way to the door and grabbed a t-shirt, hopping from foot to foot toward the door until his toes poked through the ankles of his sweatpants. Then, he groped for the doorknob as he tugged his shirt down.

When he opened it, instead of one of the queens, it was a delivery guy—unmistakably, since he had a uniform and even a cute little uniform hat.

Holding flowers.

River's head slowly tilted. Maybe they had the wrong room. Tina's new man seemed hella interested in romancing her.

Oh, shit. Or it was Zeph. They needed to have a conversation about this NSA thing. He'd seen the way Zeph pulled him in to deflect flirting at the club last night.

"River?"

"...Yes? I mean, hi. That's me." River kept his voice down

so he didn't disturb Zeph, not that anything but an elephant tap-dancing on Zeph's face could have woken him.

"These are for you."

They *were* pretty—pink and yellow daisies and white lilies and lots of cute little flowers he couldn't identify. But they were so not *him*, and Zeph ought to know that by now.

River wasn't about to turn them down, though. He smiled politely and nodded. "Um, cool. Wow. Thanks." He rested them in the crook of his arm, pushing his hair to the side and patting it into place.

The delivery guy nodded briskly and strode back to his car while River closed the door and tugged the card out of the plastic holder. He half-expected Zeph to sit up and make some comment about getting into his pants with the flowers.

But when he flicked the envelope open with his thumb and set the flowers on the table, then tugged the card out, his heart sank.

Then, it beat faster.

Loved watching you on stage, sexy. I'm thirstier than these flowers for you. Will you help me let it go?

-your big fan

And "big" was even underlined. That was edgy, bordering on creepy. No, outright creepy, he decided after rereading it a few times.

It took River a moment to realize it hadn't even come from the motel, but directly from a delivery person, which meant whoever this was knew which room he was in. None of the queens would have given that out, and they would have told him if anyone had asked which room he was in. Zeph sure as hell wouldn't.

And this wasn't Zeph's handiwork. Too creepy, right?

"Who's that for?"

Zeph was awake behind him, rolling over in bed and rubbing his eyes as he sleepily peered at River. Well, that confirmed that it wasn't him.

He swallowed. "Me. Apparently."

Zeph took a few moments to think that through, then pushed himself up. "One of the guys… girls… your friends?"

"No. That's the weird part. Here." River sat on the edge of the bed and handed over the card.

Zeph's brows drew together as he read the card, and then he looked up at River. "No idea who this is? Really?"

"Definitely not any of my friends," River confirmed. "And I assume it's not you."

Zeph snorted. "Well, I *am* thirsty for you, but I think you helped me let it go… what, twice last night? I don't need flowers to say it."

"Always the romantic," River deadpanned and snatched the card back, tossing it in the trash. "I'll give these to some random on the Strip who looks like they're having a bad day."

"Awww," Zeph drawled. Then, his brows drew together again as he half-sat, propping himself on his elbow.

River sighed. Now Zeph was going to get overprotective.

"So someone knows where you are."

River shrugged it off. "We'll just get another motel and tell them to keep it hush-hush. Reception must have told the delivery guy. No big deal." Everyone got a creepy admirer once in their life, right?

Zeph eyed him but let it go, flopping onto his back again. "Fine. I'll even haul your stuff over if you ask me nicely."

"I'm sure we can work out a deal." River batted his lashes, giving Zeph a long, slow look up and down.

That distracted Zeph perfectly.

"Huh." Zeph ran a finger up River's spine to the back of his neck. "Tell me more."

River flicked out his tongue playfully. "How about I show you?"

"Payment in advance? I like these terms."

River ran his hand along the sheets until he found Zeph's leg, then slowly up his thigh. "Only for you," he teased.

For the next nine days, it could be *sort of* true.

CHAPTER
Thirteen

ZEPH

HAULING *EVERYONE'S* STUFF WASN'T SUPPOSED TO BE PART OF that morning's deal, but nobody sucked cock as persuasively as River did.

Moving lodgings just a day into their trip was a little annoying, especially since the new place was further away from the strip, but Zeph wouldn't take River's nonchalance for an answer.

The very *least* they should be doing was moving motels. Zeph itched to get the cops involved, but River would freak the fuck out on him if he so much as breathed the word.

Honestly, he couldn't blame the guy. Zeph didn't know Vegas well enough to know the chances of getting some homophobic desk jockey, but despite his outrageous flamboyance, River didn't deliberately bash his head on that particular wall. Which made it more frustrating that trouble had found them anyway.

On the bright side, the new motel came with a perk: access to a gym just down the street.

Which sounded like the perfect break for Zeph, who

wasn't used to sharing space so intensively with so many people. Sharing the room with River was just the beginning —everyone went out for brunch together, and they were talking about hitting up one of the outlet malls or something downtown together.

They'd already made it clear that sticking around them was very optional in the mornings and afternoons until showtimes, though Zeph was starting to reconsider his plans of spending those times on his own.

But River was a lot more touchy-feely than even he realized. Zeph had forgotten his habits—like putting his hand on Zeph's shoulder and leaning into him like a wall while he was talking to other people, or touching his back or arm or hand while talking to him. He was starting to get overstimulated by the contact.

Plus, he needed to work out his frustration at not being able to do more about this creepy creeper.

The gym was set up much the same as any other, with a small free weight area and the usual machines. After a cursory glance around, Zeph chose a lat pulldown machine so he could mindlessly warm up and think.

He exchanged nods with the other guys in there who looked like they could be regulars. At least his build and size gave him instant respect in this space.

Whoever it was, the card had made it clear they'd seen River at the show last night, and they knew which room he was in. So they must have seen him, but it still wasn't enough to make him back off.

That was *not* jealousy, and he'd only defaulted to *him* because most stalkers were men, he told himself.

A stab of emotion went through his chest and he pushed out a quick breath, leaning over to push the pin into the next weight down in the stack. If he had brain space to think, he wasn't going hard enough.

He hated that River was just shrugging off the creeper problem. He didn't want River to be distraught and hide away, but the response reminded him too much of…

Fuck. Fine. His brain was going to go there, like it or not.

He rolled his head back as he counted down a rest break.

River reminded him of Anton. They'd been best friends with benefits for a few years, many years ago now—before he'd even met River the first time. God, he'd been young then.

Anton had picked up a casual stalker. Not the kind to leave dead animals on his doorstep, but the kind who showed up at his retail shop every day, and sent presents.

But Anton had been closeted, and too afraid to go to the cops, and he'd wound up dying in a car crash while trying to escape the guy when he started tailing him home.

A muscle twitched in Zeph's jaw and he gripped the bar, grunting as he pulled the bar down, widening his stance.

Fucker hadn't gotten nearly enough jail time for that.

Zeph wasn't ready to have River go through anything near what Anton did. He wanted to head trouble off at the first sight of it.

But he couldn't do anything unless River was ready to recognize the seriousness of the situation. And in fairness, River was right—so far, it had just been one bunch of flowers.

Next time, though, if there was one? Zeph wasn't going to let him get away with brushing it off and changing the subject. Even if he didn't want to go to the cops, Zeph could take matters into his own hands.

If some asshole wanted to get his hands on River and

River didn't like it, well, Zeph would find a way to break his fingers one by one.

If River wasn't going to look after himself, Zeph was going to damn well do it for him. And it had nothing to do with jealousy. He'd do the same for any damn queen in their group.

The thought snuck into the back of his mind that the fact that it was River *did* make him more passionate. But it just meant he'd be more enthusiastic about finger-breaking.

Zeph let the weights drop onto the stack and leaned over to clip into the floor for pull-ups. Time for less thought, more sweat.

CHAPTER
Fourteen

RIVER

"So, what happened this morning?"

RB had River cornered while he was applying eyeshadow, so he couldn't wiggle away and change the subject like he had all day.

River hesitated, dabbing his finger in the highlight color and examining his face in the mirror. It gave him something to watch other than RB's face, which was distinctly worried.

"Don't give me that *nothing* bullshit, either." RB kept his voice down as he leaned against the chair. He squeezed River's shoulder just firmly enough to make it clear he wasn't letting him get away from this one. "Did Zeph give you those mysterious flowers you gave that chick?"

River let out a quiet sigh. If he had a best friend other than Kyle, it was RB. "Fine, I'll spill. But don't tell the others."

"Uh oh." RB folded his arms, refusing to promise that.

River rolled his eyes. "Fine. I just got them delivered to our door... from some anonymous big fan. The card was basically like, *thanks for getting me hard, help me get off,* but in… you know, creepier, prettier words. So, keep an eye out for anything weird tonight, yeah?"

"Of course. But I like that prettier words means creepier to you," RB half-smiled, kicking his foot.

River snorted with amusement. "Well, if he wants my ass, he could come out and say it. Jesus. Saves us motel changes, and flowers are expensive to deliver, you know. Did you know a dozen roses on Valentine's—"

But RB wouldn't let him change the subject. "Are expensive, yeah. You're downplaying it."

River opened his mouth, then closed it again as he snapped his palette shut and wiped his fingers off. He half-shrugged, glancing over at the others and back to RB. "Yeah. Fine. I just don't want to alarm the others."

"Seriously, you have to tell them," RB murmured. He wasn't raising his voice and taking the choice away from him, which River appreciated, but his gaze was deadly serious.

A chill went down River's spine. Yeah, the asshole could be watching everyone. What if someone else got another bouquet and didn't say anything? What if one of the full-time girls—Glam, say—got attention next?

Not that she couldn't look after herself, but he knew the outlook was worse for trans women who lost muscle mass after hormones than guys like him in a fair fight, and this guy may not even fight fair.

That made up his mind.

"Fine," he breathed out, kicking his chair to spin toward the room. "Guys and dolls?"

Everyone knew his serious voice; the chatter died down instantly, like they'd been waiting for him to say something.

"Uh. I got this creepy admirer note and bouquet to our room this morning. That's why we changed motels."

Anna hissed through clenched teeth while Tina winced. A few of them traded looks, and then RB spoke up.

"So we gotta keep an eye out for people perving on him."

Glam tapped a five-inch stiletto heel on the floor. "If anyone tries anything…"

River bit back a smile and nodded at her. "Permission to puncture his balls. I don't know, it's probably a one-time thing, but…"

"We'll look out."

That was all they had to say about it. The mood lightened up when Tina cracked a few jokes, but there was a slight tinge of caution on the air even as they took the stage twenty minutes later.

With everyone's eyes on the crowd, plus Zeph waiting in the wings, River had never felt safer.

"I don't know if I'm glad or disappointed nobody was obviously creepy," Tina commented as she peeled off her wig and ran a hand over her hair.

"I was looking forward to a well-placed foot to break my fall during a routine," Glam agreed.

River had to laugh. "You? Fall?" He didn't think she'd even slipped during a performance before.

"Oh, I can fall on cue. Normally I keep going down…" Glam shimmied, winking at him as he groaned.

"But this isn't the all-clear," Jizzie spoke up. She'd been quiet between numbers all night, but now she was watching him closely. "People can be shady as fuck and not look like it."

River was glad the show had gone well. At least it took the sting out of the weirdness that morning, and distracted them all from his announcement. Everything seemed less important on the other side of a good performance.

"True," River agreed. "Okay, ladies. Tip time."

They pooled and split tips—which normally made the more popular and experienced queens shy away, but Tina and Glam had good business heads. They'd long since realized that pooling tips meant they could send someone around with a tip bucket to collect money from those who'd never be bold enough to tuck bills into their outfits during a well-choreographed number.

Everyone made more money this way, and tonight had been a particularly great night. There were twenties in the bucket, not just ones, and almost no loose change.

With only six of them on the road, it worked out to about two hundred bucks each, which was over double what River had hoped for.

He usually made anywhere from twenty bucks on a bad night to three hundred on a great one, but the latter nights were rare. It averaged out to about seventy, which covered his bills if he performed weekly, and the new day job he was about to get would cover rent. Food generally wasn't a problem unless he hit a run of bad nights, and he could flirt all night to get free drinks, so his lifestyle worked out.

His brain was still going over his budget for the month when he caught sight of Zeph patrolling the room, looking like he was checking the corners.

"See any suspicious packages?" River teased on the way by.

Zeph paused and eyed him, then let his gaze slip down River's body in a way that made River's knees weak. "One."

River blushed and turned his gaze to the mirror as he patted his hair back into place now that the weight of the wig was off. "Are you going to open it for me?"

Zeph's finger dragged along the top vertebra at the back of his neck, circling once before he lifted the chain of the thin gold necklace he'd worn as a prop in the last song, adjusting it so the clasp was at the back.

He raised his brows, and River nodded, heart pounding.

Those big, strong fingers moved with the same surprising delicacy River had felt against his skin and inside his body to unclasp the necklace, then dragged it down along his chest before handing it to him.

"When we get back to the motel, I'll open it nice and slowly. Just to be sure."

River barely remembered what question that answer was for, but his body didn't need the context. He couldn't get into his jeans fast enough.

Fuck, that incident was going to be a blip on the radar now. There were too many awesome things happening to stay down. In more than one sense.

River double-checked himself and tugged his sweater down over his crotch, glad he'd worn a roomy one to the venue. Some of the guys and ladies were talking about going out tonight, but all he could think about was staying in.

His eyes flickered to Zeph, who was making his way out of the room again to stand outside the door like the hot enforcer he was.

All the nightlife I need is right there.

CHAPTER

Fifteen

ZEPH

RIVER WAS OUT OF HIS MIND.

"Whipped cream? You gonna put it in your crappy instant coffee tomorrow?" Even if they were half a mile from the venue and about that far from their motel, Zeph wasn't going to let River go into the little supermarket next to the discount liquor store on his own. Just in case they were being followed.

Maybe it was a touch paranoid, but better safe than sorry.

"You'll see," River smirked.

Zeph rolled his eyes. That was all he'd said to him five minutes ago when he'd told him to stop at a supermarket, and it had taken this long to even pry out of him what exactly they were going for.

If he was going to use it during sex, well, Zeph could eat him up all night long without any fancy toppings. If the goal was to keep Zeph achingly hard in his jeans, tailing after River, half a pace behind him, like an oversized shadow... well, River was succeeding at that.

"You're just teasing now."

"I might be," River hummed.

Zeph eyed the back of River's neck. He always had a nice, clean hairline, down to maybe number one or two clippers along the back of his neck. It was prickly, yet soft to touch. He wished he could reach out here in public and do it.

Wait, why *couldn't* he?

This was Vegas, damn it, not Bumfuck, Illinois.

He caught up to River and fell into step beside him when River stopped at the dairy cooler, then raised his hand to caress the back of River's neck, pushing his hand up through the hairs there until he reached the platinum blond section.

River eyed him sideways, then reached for the whipped cream canister. "Now who's teasing?"

"I might be." Zeph shot a heavy-lidded gaze in his direction.

It worked. River shoved the whipped cream canister under his arm like a baton and marched for the register.

Zeph kept up the banter all the way back to the motel. This motel was further away from most of their venues this trip, so they had to drive now. It would be easier if he couldn't see River in his peripheral vision the whole time being so pretty.

He'd left on a sheer, light pink shade on his plump, kissable lips, and taken off his false lashes and extreme eyeshadow. Now, he just had foundation and blush or bronzer or whatever it was that made his skin fair, clear, and rosy, smooth and perfect like he'd just stepped out of a magazine. His cheekbones were sure sharp enough to cut. And if his eyes didn't already draw Zeph's attention, they certainly did when his lashes were darkened and thickened with mascara.

Jesus, Zeph had already learned a lot from hanging

around the periphery and watching River at work. Maybe he was watching him a little more than the rest of the queens.

Though River came off as self-centered and aware of his own good looks, Zeph was certain he wasn't fully aware of *how* gorgeous he was.

For the hundredth time, he dragged his attention off his lover and back to the road, turning the corner into the motel parking lot. "Thank God," he mumbled. He'd made it back without an accident from staring too hard at River.

"A little on edge there?" River murmured, his voice sultry.

Oh, he had no idea. It was just as well he thought it was purely sexual tension, and not…

Whatever the hell he felt when he looked at River.

Zeph rolled his eyes at River and grabbed the car keys, leading the way to the motel room. "Cocktease."

The clatter of metal on metal caught his attention, and he glanced over his shoulder. In answer, River was just shaking the whipped cream canister.

A rare blush burned Zeph's cheeks as he pushed the motel room door open and held it for River, who brushed slowly and deliberately by him.

When the door swung closed, Zeph grabbed River around the waist and pulled him into his chest, tucking his nose into the crook of River's neck and pushing his top aside to kiss slowly along one shoulder.

River weakened in his arms, so he tightened his grip as he licked slowly along bare skin back to his neck, then kissed behind his ear before letting him go so they could kick their shoes off.

They didn't waste time with the rest of their clothes, either. Both of them fought each other's clothes off all the way to the bed, leaving a telltale trail of fabric heaps until they hit the mattress, still kicking off their underwear.

God, Zeph ached to feel River around him, but River had other plans. The sexy blond manhandled him to the bed, then straddled him and shook the canister at him again.

"Stop wielding that like a weapon and I'll be a little more enthusiastic," Zeph grumbled as River peeled off the plastic strip.

River shot back, "Do you not want my mouth on you?" One razor-sharp brow was angled up.

Zeph swallowed hard and gave in, shaking his head. "No, I do."

"Good. Shut up, then." River tore the cap off with his teeth and spat it aside, then pressed the side of the nozzle and dragged it through the air above his breastbone, drawing a line down the center of his body all the way to the base of his cock.

The canister rolled into his side as River tossed it aside, too, and pounced like a wild animal. Their dicks pressed together at first as he lapped at his throat, but River kept himself held carefully up in the air so he didn't smear it on himself.

Yet, Zeph thought with a wicked smile to himself that River couldn't see, his open mouth too busy on Zeph's collarbone.

Jesus, that hot, wet mouth did wonders. Zeph rolled his head back into the pillow and kneaded River's shoulders as his cock begged for more of that heat on it, not the rest of him.

In time, he tried to remind himself and stay patient, but patience was hard to come by with that tongue flicking slowly at one of his nipples.

"*Fucking…* fuck," Zeph gasped, arching clear off the bed as the jolt of electric need shot straight to the tip of his cock. He bumped River's chest and strained upward toward him.

Before he could grind, River grabbed his hips and slammed him back to the bed with surprising strength. "No."

Zeph stared, open-mouthed. He'd like to think that he could have resisted that move, but nobody had tried that with him before. He honestly didn't know what to do.

River's mouth was on his stomach now, every kiss slow and deliberate as he licked the spot thoroughly, then sucked a long, slow kiss against the spot before moving down again.

He was going to have Zeph completely fucking crazy by the time he got to his cock.

"*Yeah!*" Zeph managed as River sucked the last spot of whipped cream off, just above his pelvic bone.

And then he reached for the canister again.

"You asshole," Zeph growled.

River's voice was still light, musical with amusement. His voice suited him, but goddamn, did it drive Zeph crazy at this particular second. "That changed your tune awfully quick."

"I'm gonna fuck you through the *wall* if you don't knock it off," Zeph growled.

River giggled, the noise breathless and high-pitched. "You seem to be under the impression that will discourage me."

Zeph gritted his jaw as River squirted spirals of whipped cream around each nipple, then slid back up his body, grinding absolutely deliberately against his cock with his chest and stomach.

He *was* going to snap and fucking ravish River in the next five minutes—no, three… maybe two…

River's hot tongue circled his chest in that slow, maddening spiral, until he was fucking *begging* River to suck his nipple. River just gave him a slow smirk and then lapped his tongue in a broad stroke across the nub before flicking it fast and hard, back and forth, up and down.

Zeph felt the whine of desperation escape his throat before he even heard it, and he couldn't stop the noises. He was leaking precome already, his toes curling into the bed with how hard he wanted to grab River and fuck him until River mewled his name…

River's mouth closed around his other nipple, sucking it hard into his mouth to give him a twinge of pain. That filthy tongue flicked across his nipple again, just like the other one. But this time, River kept licking, lapping, flicking, tweaking the nipple until the heat burned so hard under Zeph's skin he felt like he was in the middle of a goddamn forest fire.

Zeph had had enough.

He grabbed River by the shoulders and grunted, flipping their bodies over like River was his opponent on the mat, only with *much* less pure intentions.

"Jesus, Zeph," River whimpered, his eyes wide. "That… *hot.*"

He was losing the ability to speak? Good. That put them on even footing.

Zeph grabbed River's hands and hauled them above his head, then pinned both slender wrists together with one hand. With the other, he grabbed the discarded canister and shook it, making direct eye contact to make it clear what he meant to do.

River sucked in a slow breath and spread his legs until they weren't wrapped around Zeph's thighs. Zeph brought the canister down to squirt a line along the inside of each of his thighs.

"Fuck, fuck, fuck," River hissed, his breathing fast. His cock was swollen and red, so at least he was just as turned on and needy as Zeph.

Zeph scooted down River's body, only letting go of his wrists slowly to make it clear he was to keep his hands there.

River whimpered but nodded slightly, clasping his hands above his head.

The almost religious gesture sent a shiver down Zeph's spine, but he put it firmly in the *fuck off* thought box in his head and focused on the lines of glistening white cream waiting for him.

God, he was hungry for River.

Zeph slid down the bed and curled his thumbs around the insides of River's knees to keep his legs apart, then dragged his tongue along the inside of one smooth thigh, slowly lapping at the line of cream.

It was just as fun, if not more, to be on *this* end of pleasure, making River squirm into the bed with wordless moans. He took his sweet time licking up further and further toward his nuts, but not taking them into his mouth. He let his hot breath graze over the shaft and balls before scooting back down to the other knee to work his way up all over again.

The whole time, River kept gasping his name and swearing, but he seemed to have forgotten every other word in his vocabulary.

By the time he pushed River's knees up to his chest and held them there with one forearm under his knees, River could only manage a stuttered, desperate, "*Yes!* Zeph, f-fucking *yes…!*"

Zeph shook the can once more, and River's long, low whimper of need made his dick throb once again with the need to have that tight little hole wrapped around his shaft, milking every drop from him.

But that would come in a minute. He wanted River to *need* him so bad he couldn't breathe first.

Zeph squirted a circle of whipped cream around that tight little hole, then started lapping at the line, slowly working his way around the sensitive skin without touching the actual nerve bundle River wanted him to yet.

"Fuckfuckfuckfuck," River was moaning, his thighs twitching against Zeph's arm. His body strained and tightened, every muscle pulling tight and flexing as he managed—barely—to keep his hands where Zeph had put them.

Zeph licked across the hole, squirted a bit more cream, licked that off, and repeated a few more times.

"*Pleasemotherfuckingplease*," River growled, thrashing against his hold. His arms were starting to shift like he was about to grab Zeph's head.

Zeph tossed aside the can and ran his hand up to his shoulder to remind him who was in charge. Then, he ran his tongue around and across the opening to suck and lick the last bit of cream from that sweet, tight little hole that was clenching so tight for him before he was even inside.

"I need you, I need you, Zeph," River panted like a mantra. "Please fuck me. Please... Jesus, please, please fuck me..."

Zeph's head spun. Who the fuck could resist *that*? He needed it just as badly, and River was wet for him now. He considered letting River suck his cock first, but his nerves were so frayed he might not last more than a few minutes.

He wanted every second to be buried deep in River's sweet little ass.

So Zeph spat onto his palm and wet his cock, grunting with pleasure as the desperate skin finally got a hint of the pleasure he needed. He tightened his grip and stroked, then pushed his tongue against River's hole once more just to make sure.

"If you don't fuck me *right the fuck now*—" River growled, which was an adorable threat coming from someone as lithe and easy to keep pinned to the bed as him. His arms were even still obediently above his head.

Zeph nudged the head of his cock against River and slowly inside, taking his time to let the wet skin slide against and into the lubed-up hole.

River gasped his name, the most blissed-out expression softening his expression for a second. "Oh, *yes…*"

Zeph slid all the way in, then spat on his hand and stroked himself as he pulled out the first time to add a little more. Fuck, he'd be more worried if River weren't so wet, and if he weren't sure they were going to come in a minute or two, tops.

Apparently, River was thinking along the same lines. "*Now.*"

Zeph grabbed River's knees to push them up by his ears, doubling him up and bracing himself on his knees. Pounding into River, slowly at first, and then harder and deeper, was pure animal instinct.

Passion, need, and a touch of something primally possessive.

River was *his*, and crying *his* name, and unable to keep his hands off *him*. River finally grabbed his back and pulled him close, his nails scratching thin lines down Zeph's back.

Zeph's balls were already tightening, his whole body taut, teeth bared. He usually pulled out and stroked over his partner, but not with River. He wanted to leave him dripping with his own kind of cream.

He drove his hips into River a couple more times before his whole world narrowed and focused on *River*, on the heat and wetness of him, the stickiness of their hot skin pressed on skin, the desperation of clinging to the edge, yet wanting so hard to let go…

And then he couldn't stop himself. Orgasm hit him hard and he slammed into River, hips stuttering as he squirted his load deep inside, his balls slapping against River's skin, his heart pounding *Ri-ver, Ri-ver, Ri-ver* until the name slipped from his lips.

His head spun, his whole world spun, when he slid out of River, sweat slicking his forehead and dripping down his chest. Or maybe that was the stickiness of the whipped cream and River's mouth on him, it was hard to tell.

River's cock was flushed deep red, almost pulsating with need, and Zeph intended to fulfil it.

He slid down the bed again, careful not to touch the cock this time so he didn't hurt him with the intensity of it. Keeping River's knees against his chest, he dragged his tongue along one inner thigh, lifted his head until he made eye contact with River, then leaned in to lick that tight little hole.

Tasting his own come was pretty damn easy. He thanked his own good diet for that. The look on River's face as he swallowed the thick load, slightly sweet still with the taste of whipped cream, was absolutely fucking *mindblown*. River couldn't keep his hips still as he squirmed under his tongue.

Zeph licked his palm, wrapped his hand gently around

the aching dick right at eye level, and stroked at the same quick pace he pushed his tongue into River.

"*Zeph!*" River whimpered. Then, he thrashed up against him as he came, half-shouting Zeph's name in the hoarsest, sexiest fucking whine he'd ever heard from River's mouth.

River came *hard*, his thighs and dick and arms twitching—every goddamn part of him seizing up with pure, gorgeous, unrestrained pleasure as his own passion coated his stomach and chest in quick, hard squirts and every muscle in his body rippled.

The raw noise of ecstatic need spilling from River's lips, the way his mouth fell open as he gasped—it was almost enough to get Zeph hard again on the spot. If he could have, he would have sprung another boner for him in a heartbeat.

Zeph relentlessly milked every drop out of him until River's breathing softened, then caught with sensitivity. He loosened his grip for a few final strokes before letting go of the softening skin and running his hands down River's thighs, pulling his mouth away from the still-twitching, raw hole.

River couldn't even look at him. He brought both hands to cover his face.

"Did I just find your line?" Zeph's grin was huge. "Did *I* embarrass *you*?"

River moaned. "No. Shut up." He was slowly pulling his feet up the bed as if to curl up.

"I totally did. Jesus, you loved that."

River wouldn't say anything to that, but he also wouldn't pull his hands away from his face. Coming from the most sexual being Zeph had ever met, it was the compliment of his life.

"Oh my God," Zeph laughed richly, flopping by River's side. "I love eating you out, you know that."

"Shut uuuup."

"I'll do it *way* more often if you keep blushing like that." Zeph pinched River's cheek.

River pulled his hands away from his face to smack his hand away, so Zeph repeated it on his other cheek.

"You asshole."

"What's that about assholes?"

River looked away again, but he was laughing loudly.

Sure, he laughed a lot—with everyone, about everything—but for once, there was no posing, no sense that he was somehow guiding the interactions, no pretence.

Just the two of them tangled together, side by side, laughing about their bodies, and the pleasure that hummed through their very bones.

Zeph's head spun. He loved this. He loved it so much it almost worried him.

"Jesus, we're a mess," River laughed.

"The whipped cream was your idea," Zeph reminded him, winking. "So it's your fault."

"Blame me. Sure. I'm cool with that."

Zeph snorted. "We should shower, though." He patted River's thigh. "Will you be able to stand?"

"You don't have to carry me. But if you wanna throw me down again..." River teased, slowly pushing himself to sitting. He swayed, and Zeph kept an eye out as he sat to make sure he wouldn't have to catch him after all.

"I'll keep that in mind."

He'd learned a lot about River that night that would come in handy over the next week.

It was kind of a shame—he'd never felt like *this*, laughing and exhausted and thrilled and just deeply contented to his very bones—with any of his long-term lovers.

But a deal was a deal, and goddamn, he still had over a week to enjoy it. This was gonna be the best week of Zeph's life.

In fact, he reflected as he went ahead to turn on the shower water, it already was.

CHAPTER
Sixteen

RIVER

River knew exactly where to look: the front right pocket of his suitcase.

He'd been setting aside his cash for the last five weeks—just twenty bucks a week. For about that long, too, he'd been planning this casino day and night for their night off between shows. He was ridiculously excited, even for him.

Logically, he *knew* he didn't have a statistically great chance of winning big. The house always won.

That didn't stop the thrill of possibility from tickling his thoughts. River also knew that was the exact seduction that made people go over their limits, but he was good at sticking to a hard limit. Bringing along exactly the amount of cash he intended to gamble with was one surefire way to stop when he was out of money.

But if he *did* happen to win big, there was a pro makeup kit he'd had his eye on for several months now. With his new work discount, it was just about in reach if he came out even a couple hundred bucks ahead. Otherwise, he'd work at saving up all over again and get the kit the slow but sure way.

He perched on the bathroom counter as he dabbed foundation onto his nose and cheeks almost without thought. The routine was easy as anything. He wasn't going for a full drag look tonight—the theatrical highlights looked good from a distance but not up close.

A simpler evening look like he usually put on after a show would flatter him but not look garish to anyone with an unbiased eye.

Zeph had already insisted on coming along, not that it was a chore to have his hunky arm candy around. River knew it was also for protective reasons, and he couldn't lie… he kind of felt hot about that, too. And touched.

"You make that look easy," Zeph commented as he approached the bathroom doorway.

River was in the final stages, choosing his lip shade. He paused and raised an eyebrow, glancing at him in the mirror. "It *is* easy, once you learn your face."

"I know my face."

"Do you know where to contour?"

"Uh." Zeph shrugged. "Wherever's not bruised?"

River cracked a smile. "Good point." He chose a nice dark red with a hint of purple undertones and swiped a cotton Q-tip across it to build up some product, then started applying it to his lips without liner. He leaned into the mirror to see the line more clearly.

Zeph leaned there and watched, his head tilted as he looked at the array of what had to look like mysterious tools still lined up on the counter.

When River was done with his lips, he blotted them on tissue and double-checked that he hadn't smudged anything, then smiled. "You wanna try some?"

"*Me?*" Zeph exclaimed. It was like River had suggested he try whipping up a six-course gourmet meal.

"I'll do it for you, duh."

Zeph stared at him for a moment, then looked at himself. "I dunno. I'd be pretty ugly."

"Oh, shut up," River snorted. Everyone thought that until they'd had *his* hands on their face. Makeup could do wonders for not just appearance, but self-confidence. It could highlight or deemphasize features, even change a person's whole demeanor and behavior.

That was the part most guys didn't get—just like most women, River didn't put it on for *their* benefit. It was his own creativity, a blend of art and science, a skill he'd honed over years through trial and error.

For some guys, that first time with a simple coat of foundation to cover their spots or lipstick to draw eyes was transformational.

And Zeph wasn't femmephobic, thank God, or River would ditch him here and now. He didn't recoil at the suggestion of makeup with a sneer or disbelief. It was more surprise in his expression.

"I... You can put on a little. Enough other people can't tell."

That was the single most common request of anyone just trying makeup for the first time, especially men. Doubly especially big, strong guys like Zeph. River had fully expected it, so he smiled and nodded without missing a beat. "All natural," he promised.

Zeph eyed him but came to sit on the closed lid of the toilet, folding his arms. "What do I do?"

"Sit there and try not to flinch when I approach your eyes with sharp instruments."

The worry that creased his brow for a moment made River laugh.

"I promise I've only stabbed a few eyeballs—"

Zeph suspiciously glared. "A few."

"And they deserved it," River told him.

"Uh huh. Was it with your dick?"

River cracked up and nearly dropped his concealer. "No laughing, either. Or smiling. Keep your face neutral."

"Hmph." Zeph let his expression soften to neutral and closed his eyes.

Perfect. River got a chance to stand back and examine him for a few moments. Zeph's face was angular like his own, but filled out in different spots. His jaw was wider, his nose less angular, and his eyebrows were thicker.

The least noticeable kind of makeup would probably be to even his skin tone with some foundation and concealer, and maybe add a shade of lipstick that would tint his lips slightly, but not dramatically. If Zeph approved, he could add a hint of eyeliner—or guyliner, he thought with a quiet snort—and contour just a bit.

"Given up on me?" Zeph smirked.

"I'm thinking. Hush." River patted his cheek, then pulled back. "All right."

It didn't take long to find his foundation shade, and concealer was easy—luckily, his skin fell within the range of the supplies River carried for everyone else. That much alone made a drastic difference for a lot of people, especially when he cheated and added just a bit of bronzer before Zeph could notice.

Then he went on to the lips, getting them buffed with some lip scrub and a tissue before he applied a foundation and pale shade that didn't contrast his natural lip tone too much.

"Eyeliner?"

Zeph cracked an eye open. "Really?"

"Think My Chemical Romance."

Zeph snorted with laughter and closed his eyes again. "If you must." As everyone did, he flinched the first few times River approached with his eye pencil, but then he settled down and let River draw a subtle, light gray line.

Oh, God, yes.

When he pulled back to admire his handiwork, River's eyes widened.

Jesus, he looked like an eight or a nine when he rolled out of bed, but all of a sudden, Zeph looked like… well, a *model*.

"Done?" Zeph asked, and River realized he'd just been staring speechlessly. *Speaking of thirsty, Jesus.*

"Oh. Yeah. Yeah, you're done." River patted his shoulder and stood back, watching as Zeph rose to his feet and tentatively approached the bathroom mirror.

For a moment, he stared—and then he smiled. It was an instinctive reaction, too quick to be calculated. His cheeks rounded, his eyes crinkled, and he grinned into the mirror. "I…"

He likes it. River nearly bounced on his toes, but tried to contain his excitement as he clasped his hands. "Hm?"

"I actually like it."

"No need to sound surprised," River teased. He couldn't keep his gaze off Zeph's face, too, though.

Damn, the eyeliner was the perfect touch. Subtle enough that if you weren't looking for it, it wouldn't pop, but bold enough to make him look confident and twice as handsome.

Zeph looked hot enough to make River briefly consider skipping the casino… but that makeup kit was calling to him.

"Come on, let's go, or we'll never make it," River grinned.

Zeph raised his brows and laughed. "You like it that much?"

River didn't answer, just winked before he flicked off the bathroom light and sauntered for the front door of the motel room.

They were right on time to meet the other queens in front of Glam and Tina's room, and then they set off to walk to the casino not more than a quarter mile away. Some were in drag, some not. River was the only one who'd outright call himself nonbinary, so going out like this was the norm for him.

It was one of those afternoons where everything just seemed to fall into place. Everyone included Zeph by now in their jokes and anecdotes, and he laughed along with the rest of them.

Time seemed immaterial; for this afternoon, none of them had a care except enjoying life and each other's company.

The penny slots were their first stop to blow twenty bucks each, and once that was gone, they split up into three groups—for now, some headed for the video arcade, others for blackjack, and the third group to play roulette.

Zeph, River, and Tina all headed for the video roulette tables, since they were cheaper to buy into than the physical tables right now. Plus, with this section to themselves, they could make all the dirty jokes they wanted about the ball, and covering the board with their claims.

"I can't believe you said that," Zeph groaned at Tina.

"You don't know me half as well as you think, then," Tina

teased. "That's all right. You can get to know me." But she gave a quick sideways glance at River as she said it, as if to make sure it was okay.

Oh, boy. They all think I'm with Zeph.

But as the roulette wheel spun and his eyes were drawn to the board again, River tried to hold back his smile.

It felt a bit like his life right now.

Two to one says it doesn't work out, but I'm having a hell of a good time while I can.

CHAPTER
Seventeen

ZEPH

"No, no, reel in that one!"

Somehow, the whole group had ended up gathered around a video slot machine, arguing about which lobsters Tina should choose for her bonus round.

In an effort to stay out of the debate, Zeph had grabbed himself a beer, but from the sounds of it, they were no closer to deciding which lobsters to choose.

He settled down at a terminal nearby, keeping half an ear on the conversation as he fed five bucks into the machine.

"We should ask River. He seems to be an expert."

River scoffed. "At lobsters?"

"You *know* who I'm talking about," Glam scoffed right back at him. "RB? Back me up."

RB gave a noncommittal hum.

"Oh, RB knows something he's not sharing. Selfish."

River snorted with laughter. "I'm going to get a drink, since the waitress seems to have developed an allergy to obnoxious fags."

The word still made Zeph wince, but he could see exactly

why River used it. It took away the last vestige of anyone's power to hurt him with it. It gave him a sense of community with all the flamboyant personalities in this group... the bonding of social exiles.

In a way, Zeph was a little jealous. He pulled the terminal handle and tried to shut down that line of thought as the digital wheels spun.

He didn't need a word for himself. He was fine without labels, he told himself. One like that? Yeah, he wasn't sure he could even use it for himself.

"What can I threaten RB with?" That was Tina again.

RB snorted. "There's nothing in the world you can do to me that I can't do to myself, hon."

"I beg to differ," Tina teased. "Come on, what's with the two of them?"

"Your guess is as good as mine. He looks happy, though," RB told her.

"Really happy," Dixie chimed in. "Mind you, he's been looking forward to this for ages."

"You think they're...?"

"What? Already? No."

"River nearly tore your head off for flirting with him," Anna chimed in.

Zeph's cheeks were hot as he upped his bet to the max lines so he could burn through his cash faster and take a stroll. Unfortunately, he was winning.

Gossip was inevitable, they both knew that. They hadn't been trying to hide it, and they *had* been taking every opportunity to fuck.

But the way they were talking... it made him wonder what exactly River had told them, if anything. Especially RB, who seemed to know more than he was letting on.

Had River made it out to be more than it was?

The possibility made Zeph uneasy. He kept half an ear on their idle speculation until it drifted to other subjects, but the thoughts the gossip had brought up weren't so easy to dismiss.

Was it really the idea of River wanting more that made him uneasy? Or was it the possibility that *he* wanted more with River?

He couldn't really tell which. Maybe all of this was wishful thinking because he wanted River to fall for him, and this whirlwind fling to turn into...

What, exactly? A boyfriend who picked him up at the gym after training? Who put up with his weird eating habits, and taped up his bruises?

He couldn't wrap his head around what a relationship with River would even look like.

When he finally ran out of money, he got up and wandered through the rows of machines, glancing at the people who seemed glued to them.

Then, Zeph stopped dead in his tracks.

There. It's him.

There was no mistaking him, even all these years later. Zeph froze, like the world was suddenly pulling back from him, growing around him, leaving him small and helpless and wanting to be unconscious. Or dead. Anything but this.

"Father Peters. I appreciate you taking such good care of my boy. He's been in need of some guidance since the Lord blessed us with him."

Zeph—that wasn't his name back then, but it didn't matter anymore—stayed very still, silent. Hands folded in his lap, eyes down.

The priest's feet shuffled under the desk, and his palms were sweating.

His head spun.

Not again, he wanted to say. Not again, don't leave me with him.

But the last time he'd asked that, his new foster father had lectured him about speaking of a man of God that way. He'd gotten on his knees to pray with him for forgiveness.

George—he wouldn't call his foster father Dad, that was for his real dad—saw something in his brother, Father Peters, that Zeph couldn't.

Or maybe he didn't see something that Zeph could.

Or maybe they both saw each other for who they were, and Zeph was trapped between them.

What George did to him was his own fault. Father Peters had told him that. He wasn't ever, ever to tell a soul, except Father Peters, because Father Peters understood, and he would help him.

He'd tuned out the rest of the conversation. The door closed.

Father Peters stood up like he had all the time in the world, but the tension in the room was unbearable. Thick. Hot.

Just like...

No. No, no, no.

A broad hand closed around his shoulder, and Zeph's eyes closed on their own. The priest was speaking, but he'd tuned him out.

Zeph's mind was fixed on one fact that made him choke with fear: he wanted to burn for eternity. It would be better than what was coming now.

Fuck. Zeph couldn't do it. He'd shut down. He recognized that fact, objectively. He couldn't get the memories out of his head, and he couldn't talk to the man while they were there.

George didn't see Zeph—he was able to duck behind the

last row of machines, then steered around them until he was half the casino floor away from the man.

Zeph felt small, like everyone who brushed against him was a threat. It had been a long, *long* fucking time since he'd felt like that.

Finding an exit door in a casino was like finding his balls in a pair of old boxers, but somehow he was outside in the darkening evening. He gulped cool, fresh air, the cigarette smoke still burning his throat and lungs.

Or maybe that was nausea. He fought it back, leaning against the side of the building and rolling his head back as he coughed.

"Hey, you taking a breather?" It was River. Not only could he tell from his footsteps and his light voice, but the way a warm weight pressed into his side. River leaned into him like he could even support himself right now. "Smoky in there. Jesus."

"Yeah, and a break. I wanna be alone, if you don't mind."

River was quiet for a moment, and the weight pulled back from Zeph a moment later, giving him a chance to breathe. "Oh. Yeah, we're pretty raucous, sorry. Come, uh, find me when you're ready."

Zeph nodded tightly.

River paused there a few moments longer before his footsteps receded and the door clicked shut again.

Hope I didn't scare him off.

But if he had, it was just as well. It was nobody's job to deal with Zeph's fucked-up brain.

Eighteen

RIVER

IT WAS WEIRD TO WAKE UP DISCONTENTED. EVERY MORNING OF their trip, River had woken up lazy and satisfied, but still itching for another round.

But the sex last night had been... lackluster, that was a good word. Not *bad*, not awkward or painful, never that. But almost... out of touch?

River still wasn't sure what was wrong. At the casino, he'd spotted Zeph off by himself, happily playing the slots. Then he'd gone outside for fresh air and alone time. He'd come back in and all had seemed well for that evening until they left, but when they'd tumbled into bed together, it had happened all over again: one minute he'd been fine, and the next he'd been withdrawn and quiet.

Afterward, drifting off to sleep, he'd seemed upset, but he'd pretended to be asleep and River had respected his privacy.

Zeph still didn't seem to want to talk about it. As they went out for brunch, then came home and got ready to meet the management of their venue that night, Zeph was a silent shadow.

So River started joking, chatting about this and that, trying to draw Zeph out of his head if he wouldn't talk about what was going on in it. Glossing over it came easy to him, and it seemed like the best course of action.

"What's the gym here like?"

"Not much to speak of," Zeph admitted. "But it does the job. There's free weights, and as long as you have those, you're set." When River made a face, Zeph eyed him. "Don't tell me you do cardio."

"I like biking."

Zeph snorted. "It's a waste of calories. It doesn't even burn those effectively, either."

"Uh huh," River grinned. After the last day of being withdrawn, he liked seeing him worked up about *something*.

They picked up Glam on the way by, and she and Zeph chatted about the gym all the way to the car. As Zeph drove, he explained the benefits of different types of weight lifting —high impact, resistance, something something.

Glam was arguing that something called "hit" was better, and Zeph insisted even that was overcomplicating things. That was about the gist of what River understood, but he didn't need to know more.

Oh, God. Now he was understanding how his best friend, Kyle, tuned out pretty men just to hear the sound of their voices. *I need to update him on all of... this... as soon as we're back.* But the thought of returning to L.A. wasn't a welcome one.

"Is it this place?" Zeph asked, breaking his reverie as his lover and driver squinted down a one-way street. "Fucking one-ways."

"You could reverse up it."

Zeph's lips twitched. "You can find innuendo there, I'm sure."

"Look for it yourself."

"There's *definitely* innuendo there," Glam snickered.

As Zeph circled the block, River laughed. "It's gonna be one of those days, huh?"

It didn't take long before Zeph found a parking lot a block away, grabbing a ticket on the way in. He tried to wave them ahead but they stuck around, waiting for him to be ready before they set off for their newest venue.

"Is this the swishy cocktail bar?"

"No. That's the night after tomorrow, for closing night," Glam reminded River.

"Duh. Right."

"Button-down shirt swishy?" Zeph asked, clearly listening in to their conversation.

Glam winked at him. "Darling, you'd fit in anywhere in a mankini."

River choked back a laugh at the look on Zeph's face as he worked through that one in his head. "Not mandatory, though."

"Shh, no, you're supposed to tell him it is! Work with me," Glam hissed.

Zeph chuckled deeply and shook his head. "You two." They turned the corner to the bar, and River felt that familiar shiver of anticipation.

It took longer than usual for him to hit it off with the manager on duty. Flynn wasn't saying something. Soon, Flynn excused himself and headed to the office to see about arrangements for the night.

River leaned on the bar and tapped his nails against the

counter, leaning over to check behind it. A tidy bar usually meant a decent club; similarly, a bar with beer splashes and glued-down bottle caps before the place opened was never a good sign.

This place was all right, actually. Not slick, but clean and well-kept, despite being on the shabby end of chic.

Glam had dragged Zeph off to introduce her to the bouncer by the time Flynn returned.

"So, uh," Flynn addressed River, tugging at the top fastened button of his white shirt—the third one down—as he approached.

"That sounds like bad news." River wasn't impressed at being made to wait for whatever the hell this was about.

"I guess so. It looks like we're double-booked tonight."

River continued staring evenly at Flynn and raised one brow slowly, a move he'd perfected to make guys squirm.

"So, uh," Flynn said, tugging at his collar again, "you can't perform tonight." Flynn raised a hand as if to dismiss him with a casual wave.

River heard Zeph and Glam approaching by the way their breaths caught, and Glam made a noise of protest.

River raised a hand slightly to tell them he'd handle it. And boy, would he ever.

Whatever had upset Zeph, hopefully this wouldn't be enough to make him shut down again today. He didn't want his lover to see him getting nasty, but if that was what it took to make a venue honor its booking...

River ran through the numbers in his head. At this hour, it would be impossible to find another venue—even in Vegas. They were relying on the income—less so him than some of the others who didn't have full-time jobs.

And even if they didn't need the venue, he'd tear this guy's head off for thinking he could shoo them away like irritating queeny barflies.

Sorry, Zeph. You're about to get a crash course in the scene.

CHAPTER
Nineteen

RIVER

"—AND WHAT'S MORE, YOUR SHOES *DO NOT* MATCH YOUR BELT."

Zeph squeezed River's shoulder and leaned in to murmur, "You were doing better before that tangent. Back to the subject."

Right. Yes. River fanned himself with a hand, spreading his stance as he glared at Flynn.

Flynn's weight shifted to one foot as he folded his arms and gave River a cursory up-and-down with obligatory lip curl. "Girl—"

"Amazingly, even less impressive than your belt is your failure to uphold your contractual obligations. So I encourage you to *check your diary again,*" River finished, jutting out his chin at the manager. He rapped his nails on the counter, hard and rapid clicks like machine gun fire.

His chest was tight with anger. How *dare* Flynn try to flick him away like some unwanted promoter? They'd booked this place specifically, and if they were going to be denied, he wanted a damn good reason.

Frankly, half of his anger wasn't even about the situation.

He was irritated with Zeph for not manning up and talking about his feelings. Whatever was going on in his head, hiding it away wasn't helping either of them.

Flynn wordlessly turned and strode for the office. Within moments, before River could even finish the rhythm he was drumming on the bar top, he was back. Another, older guy followed him.

To his credit, the guy looked clueless but nice enough. He ran a hand back through his hair as he looked between the three of them, then at Flynn. "I understand there's confusion over booking dates?"

"There's no confusion," River told him. "A booking was made and confirmed for our show. And now Flynn tells us there's a double booking? I'm very unimpressed with the professionalism here."

"Oh, well. Is there?" the guy—maybe the owner—asked Flynn.

Flynn looked uncomfortable and nodded. "Yeah. But I told them they can't perform tonight, and uh, this guy turned into some whiny bitch."

"Flynn." The owner's voice was sharp and reprimanding, and River fought back the urge to grin. He hadn't wanted to add that to his list of things to lecture Flynn on. "Who's the other booking?"

Flynn didn't make eye contact. "Uh, the band I told you about—"

"With your nephew?"

River sucked in a breath, covering his lips with the tips of his fingers after a moment when he realized that had been audible.

"Well..." The owner seemed to hesitate.

Oh, *hell*, no.

"Surely if they'd booked first, our booking wouldn't have been taken," River interjected, leaning in over the bar. "And we'd have gone to some other bar that actually hosted us courteously. We might be a bunch of sissy queens, but we bring in crowds. You know we do."

He wasn't even trying to be polite, his lips a narrow line, his shoulders tense. Then, he went for the kill.

"It looks an awful lot like nepotism—don't look surprised I can say words more than two syllables, while I'm being a catty little motherfucker, Flynn—if you let his nephew push us out."

The owner looked at Flynn, and River knew he'd won before he even said a word. "I'm afraid we usually go with the first-booked act."

"Dirk—"

"We can work something out," River told Flynn. He hated making a peace offering, but there were a hundred ways Flynn could ruin their night or their tips if he didn't. "Shows *always* start late. What time were they supposed to be on?"

Dirk saw his point. "They could open for them," he nodded. "Or play live music for some of your songs…"

"Oh, nuh uh." River held up a hand. They weren't going to risk some horrible band ruining the soundtrack. Good tunes were *critical*. "I'll compromise on the opening, but not that."

He realized a moment later that technically, Glam was supposed to be doing the negotiations. But when he glanced at her, she was standing back, drumming her fingers on her chin and looking amused. Zeph was staring at him.

"Fine." Flynn looked slightly less unhappy than he had a minute ago, but his expression as he reached out to shake hands with River and mumble a half-apology were anything but apologetic.

Oh, well. There was nothing he could do to River that would catch him by surprise. Especially not with Zeph watching his back.

When Flynn and Dirk disappeared for a moment to talk, River sprawled against the counter and winked. "Result."

"That… was…" Zeph trailed off. Then, he shook his head. "You actually bared your teeth there." He gestured at Flynn. "And *he*… I mean, I knew gay clubs get… you know… dramatic…"

River snorted. "Understatement."

"But… did he actually imply you're all, um… a bus full of prostitutes? And then you insulted his *shoes*? And his… his… contractual obligations?" He looked stunned, like he was retelling himself the story just to be sure he'd heard everything right. "I think I should have punched him. I just wasn't sure when."

As Glam snickered, River joined in and giggled. Oh, if Zeph thought *that* was drama, he hadn't seen *anything* yet. All he'd done was apply a little bit of force at the right moments to get their way.

"Welcome to showbiz, darling."

Twenty

ZEPH

There was a lot to learn about self-described queeny fags.

Not that Zeph would have described them as that, and the words they threw around still made him wince, but none of them seemed to particularly care like Zeph did.

So he tried to set aside his expectations and learn from them. The stereotypes about brunch were true, but some of these queens really only did it as a performance art, and were gay men just about as butch as Zeph the rest of the time. Others were women full-time, and the guys respected them.

All of them sniped at each other in ways that Zeph would have taken as brewing for a fight, but it actually seemed loving when he watched them for long enough. It was when they *didn't* make catty yet affectionate comments that he knew something was up.

And they looked out for each other in ways that even Zeph, assigned to their physical safety, couldn't do. Hell, he'd seen the way they watched the audience on River's behalf and kept him distracted after the flower incident.

The stressful middle of their run had passed, and now they were about to finish their last show. The emotion was palpable.

Zeph was going to miss them. He kind of hoped he'd be invited to hang out with them again sometimes. Not every night, but maybe once in a while. He wouldn't have thought he'd be sad to see the tour end, but it *was* fun, and sometimes touching, and... well. A not-small part of it was River.

As Zeph scanned the crowd, he didn't see anything out of place. A happy audience, growing a little musically fatigued but still hanging on every word of this final group number.

He slipped away for a quick check backstage, ducking into the dressing room.

Where a man froze in the middle of the room like he'd been caught in action.

This was a small bar with a smaller staff room they were using as a dressing room, everyone in each other's personal space.

But this guy wasn't a staff member; Zeph had memorized all their faces, like usual, before the show. He was out of place, and Zeph stood straighter to glare at him on instinct. He didn't *feel right*.

The guy avoided his gaze, mumbled an apology, and escaped. Zeph let him duck around him to trot down the hall and back to the club floor.

It was only then Zeph realized he could have been some guy looking for a hookup, or a boyfriend of a staff member or someone. *Jeez. Relax, already.*

His gaze landed on a vase on the tiny makeshift makeup table.

Dead flowers. Papery roses, dried out, to be precise. And...

Shit, is that?

It was: a dead mouse.

"What the *fuck?*" Zeph exclaimed so loudly he was surprised he didn't cause a ruckus on the floor.

He burst out of the staff room and scanned the crowd, pacing the edges and checking by both bars.

Nothing. The guy was gone. He couldn't find the motherfucker. Either he'd just fled the club like a bat out of hell, or he was hiding in the hundred or so people crammed into the tiny place and keeping his face well-hidden.

Zeph bared his teeth, cursing himself for letting him go.

He marched backstage again, waiting until the applause died down and the queens started strutting around the curtain to the little section of the bar behind the stage.

"Guys." Zeph's voice was quiet but serious, catching everyone's attention. He looked apologetically at River. "Don't go in there for a sec."

River's cheeks paled, and three of them instantly flocked around him, gripping his arm and touching his shoulder.

Satisfied they'd take care of him if he fainted or something, Zeph ducked back into the staff room to take a cellphone photo or two of the setup.

Before he could figure out if he should move that shit so they could get back in here and wouldn't have to see it or leave it intact as evidence, there was a muffled gasp from behind him.

"That motherfucker!"

Everyone was crammed in the doorway, craning their heads to peer around his shoulder. River was front and center.

Zeph sighed and rolled his eyes. "You never listen to me."

"Good. Wouldn't want you getting cocky," River told him, but his smile was faint and forced.

Zeph slid his arm around River's shoulders to comfort him and pull him into his chest to emphasize his next words. "You *have* to report this."

"I don't want to."

"I know," Zeph murmured, then nodded at it. "There's a dead mouse there, too."

"Jesus *fuck*." River's head snapped up as he squinted at the table on the other side of the room again, then leaned slowly into Zeph, pressing his hand against Zeph's chest.

Zeph covered River's hand with his own. "Trust me. Please."

"Okay."

He'd won, but it was a hollow victory. River's sigh was slow and resigned. Zeph *hated* seeing that in his face, hearing it in the sigh, even feeling it in his posture. He wanted to break that asshole's face even more now.

"Okay. I'll call the cops now," Zeph murmured, shifting to grab his phone.

Glam took charge of River and Anna went to clear off a spot on the couch for him.

He'd never imagined calling the cops before.

Ever.

It was surprisingly easy. An hour later, there was a bored-looking rookie pacing the room while a forty-something guy with a moustache and an uncomfortable smirk asked them all what they knew about this "supposed stalker" and pretended to take notes.

Before Tina could enact the murder in her expression, the others shuffled her away, and Zeph waved them all off except River.

His heart was already sinking.

"We'll have to explore the avenues here, of course. When did you say you were driving back to L.A.?"

"Tomorrow," River mumbled. He was doing that thing where he stood so close to Zeph that he could feel his body heat, then swayed toward him.

Zeph braced himself and slid his arm around River's shoulders. He watched the cop's eyes drag slowly along the arm to Zeph's face, then snap down to his notepad again. He watched the shifting weight again.

He knew how to read body language. Hell, he didn't have to be an expert to see this guy wanted nothing to do with this. At best, it was going in the round file the minute he got back to the station.

"That's all for now. You can, er," the cop gestured with his pen at the vase.

"Just throw the evidence out," Zeph quipped, his lip tugging up into a half-smile. He wanted the asshole to know he knew what he was up to.

River's voice was faint. "Thanks for your time, officer." When the guy left the room, River flipped him off with both hands.

Zeph managed to crack a smile and guided River to sit down again, then found a trash can to toss everything into.

Disgusting little creep. Thank God they were leaving town tomorrow.

"Well, that's going nowhere," River muttered. Zeph could tell it took all his self-restraint not to add a *told you so*.

Zeph heaved a sigh. "I'm sorry. I hoped... you know." He didn't know why, honestly. He'd never really believed there was help out there for him, especially from the cops.

But for River? He wanted the heavens to open up and offer some kind of comfort—protection—justice.

And when they didn't, he was spitting mad.

Glam ducked inside again, followed by the others. "That's going nowhere fast, is it?"

"And they couldn't even send their hot young studs to a lady's aid." Dixie managed to make River smile.

As Zeph watched them coax him into more smiles, then the occasional laugh, he leaned against the wall and shoved his hands into his pockets, unable to help feeling like he'd let River down.

I want to...

But there was nothing more Zeph could do except wait for River to take off his stage makeup and be ready for his ride back to the hotel.

So he waited.

CHAPTER

Twenty~One

RIVER

Fuck everyone, pretty much.

That went for the creepy fuckers who thought he owed them favors because he smiled and winked at them in the audience, and fuck the cops who didn't care if some guy was trying to scare him.

As he stepped past Zeph into their motel room, River threw his bag down next to the door. He drew a breath to rid himself of those thoughts. He still had one thing to enjoy.

For one more night, anyway.

Jesus, he wasn't ungrateful, or even disappointed. River knew their sex had been fun, inventive, mind-blowingly hot, and best of all, as frequent as possible. And he loved every minute of that.

But even before this creepy threat, he'd been intensely aware that their limited time together was drawing to a close, and this was the last night of their agreement.

Back to L.A., and the real world, and not being able to get a guy to look at him as worth more than one hot night.

Not like they thought he was smart and interesting; not

like they wanted to stroke his skin after sex just to make him smile; certainly not like they wanted to punch anyone who even looked at him just a little wrong.

Fuck. River was emotionally raw just thinking about saying goodbye to Zeph again. Frustration knotted in his chest as he peeled off his blouse and skirt, kicked off his Converse, and hit the bed in just his underwear.

"I need a shower."

Zeph was undressing more leisurely, sitting on the other bed. "Room for two?"

River eyed him, tilting his head against the pillow for a better angle. Watching the tattoos ripple on his forearms as he unbuttoned was fascinating. Every time he worked the muscles of his fingers or hands, his tattoos shifted slightly, drawing eyes to them. He hadn't asked about the meaning behind any of them, but he found himself curious.

"Well?" Zeph prompted. "If you keep looking at me like that, I'm going to infer your answer."

River burst out laughing, dragging his eyes back up to Zeph's pretty face. That was just as appealing to gaze at. "Sorry. Yeah, you can invite yourself in." He pushed himself to his feet and padded to the bathroom, wiggling his ass when he got to the doorway. "If you can resist."

"I can't." Zeph's voice was close, and River gulped back his gasp when he looked over his shoulder and found Zeph halfway across the room already.

Zeph wanted River as much as he wanted Zeph. He was certain of it. He just didn't know how to *ask*—how to bring it up.

Hey, so, our ten-day deal? I kind of fucked up. I want you for longer now. I don't do that with guys... I don't get attached. But I just did.

Would Zeph want that? What if this was all just confined to the bounds of… whatever this trip was? Maybe Zeph would shut down and move again. Christ only knew what would happen the moment they got back to L.A..

But River had already made the fatal mistake: he was in way, way too deep. Like the first time, but ten times worse now, his heart was in it.

Moments after he slipped into the shower, Zeph joined him.

Even their playful shower, scrubbing wet hands across each other's soapy bodies, couldn't get his mind off his thoughts—that this was the last shower he'd share with Zeph, and he wasn't sure he could deal with that.

Fuck, fuck, fuck.

They were both hard by the time they finished scrubbing each other clean, and sidling up to Zeph to make their hard cocks bump came as second nature.

Zeph growled and picked him up, his grip firm on River's slippery skin. "No teasing today."

"No," River agreed in a quick breath, looping his arms around Zeph's neck. "None."

Zeph grabbed the lube after dumping River on the bed, one hand loosely curled around his own hard-on. "Ideas?"

The possibilities blew River's mind: he could ask Zeph to jerk off for him, that was always hot. Or he could make him fuck him and finish on his stomach for him to see. Or suck him off and then fuck those pretty lips himself…

Zeph took advantage of his momentary silence and tossed the lube next to him, then hit the bed with his face at roughly chest-level. That, in itself, was a clue as to what was next.

"Oh, fuck," River whimpered as a lip closed around his

nipple, and Zeph sucked it hard. True to his word, though, Zeph didn't draw out the teasing—he just sucked for a few moments more, then switched to his other nipple, then went up to his collarbone for a gentle nip or three before methodically kissing his way down the center of his stomach.

Before he knew it, that hot mouth pressed open-mouthed, hot kisses and licks against his shaft to the tip, then wrapped around it. Slowly, Zeph sucked his hardness into his mouth and throat.

River raised his hand to his mouth and bit the side of his fist, but the noise of need and approval vibrated through his chest. He fought to keep his hips flat on the bed.

Zeph's hand and mouth slid to the base of his dick and Christ, River wanted to memorize that feeling in case he never felt it again.

His chest tightened, and it was a good thing Zeph took his mind off it. He swiped his tongue along the sensitive spot on the underside of his shaft, squeezing him in his hand as he pulled his mouth up, then pushed back down again to engulf him in wet heat.

"Fuck, yes," River panted, his nerves lighting up from head to toe. He wanted Zeph's mouth everywhere on him—head to toe. But this was the most sensitive, raw part of him, and they weren't patient enough for foreplay today, so it would have to do.

The charge of need was building under River's skin. His stomach was tight, his fingers curled into the sheets as he squeezed his eyes shut.

I want him. All I want is him. River managed—barely—to translate that on the way out of his mouth. "Now," he breathed out. "Fingers."

Oh, fuck, those broad finger pads swiping across the

sensitive parts of him, not so deep inside but feeling like it, made his toes curl. As Zeph pushed his fingers in and out, River heard just how ragged Zeph's breathing was.

River snuck a glance at that swollen, reddened cock head and shuddered. *He's so turned on, too.* He wanted more than this—he wanted *that* in him.

"That's enough. More than enough," he grumbled. "I thought we weren't teasing."

Zeph leaned down to press a kiss against his lips. "It's fun listening to you."

Oh. Oh, my God. River's cheeks flushed and he closed his eyes.

Zeph's laugh was rich, if quiet. "That embarrasses you, too? How you squirm under me when I touch you? God, it's so unrestrained. It's the hottest thing."

"Shut up," River moaned, but his heart was pounding with pleasure. Every word turned him on, especially with Zeph's husky, hoarse voice whispering against his lips between gentle but determined kisses.

Zeph's hand cupped his cheek, but after a moment, he relented and slid his fingers out.

River waited, eyes closed, thighs trembling with need, trying to wrap his head around how painfully empty he felt. At last, the thick, warm pressure eased into him, stretching him, filling him tightly but perfectly.

This was what he needed.

River was aware of it, but he couldn't stop it: he rolled his head back, baring his throat as he cried out in pleasure. God, the momentary sting was nothing compared to the ripple of pleasure at the cock head sliding along the spot inside him that most needed attention.

Zeph sensed what he needed: though his first few

thrusts were slow and careful, his pace was intense within seconds. Rough, slow forward snaps of his hips drove his arousal deep into River's body, their bodies locked together.

Into his body, into his mind, into his heart.

River choked back another noise, leaning up, and Zeph pressed him back down with a kiss, soothing him and muffling his noises. Zeph's lips were warm and wet and hard against his, his teeth sucking River's lips into his own, his tongue slipping into River's mouth to tease River's.

Yes! River managed a moan to that effect when Zeph gave him a second to breathe, and then Zeph's teeth were on his neck, grazing his ear, nipping behind it…

Fuck, he was burning up, sweating, damp with precome as his cock throbbed with the need for attention. When he finally slipped his hand between their bodies, Zeph moaned. "That's right, baby. Want you feeling good."

"I do," River gasped. "Fuck, I do. Ohhh." His own palm felt like too much stimulation at first, but it only took a few jerks of his hand before he had a rhythm down—hard, yet still tender.

Like Zeph, like the rhythm Zeph pounded into him with, like their whole damn relationship.

It wasn't a sudden thought, but one he'd been pushing to the bottom of his mind all week, but now too impossible to ignore: this was more than sex. It was lovemaking.

And Zeph was kissing his throat, licking slowly up it until he reached his chin, pressing tiny kisses along his jaw until he reached his mouth again and kissed hard, open-mouthed.

River was the first to get his tongue into Zeph's mouth, injecting into it all the desperation that tightened his body and narrowed his mental focus. He strained up against

Zeph's body, and when Zeph's hand covered his own on his shaft, he gladly slid it away to let Zeph have all of him.

Zeph's hand was tighter than his own, rougher, but the exact tightness, texture, and rhythm of a man's hand on his dick was like a door knock—unique, impossible to forget even after years.

River whimpered again into Zeph's mouth, trying to gasp a warning. He was so aroused that he started clenching around Zeph.

The edge was *too* fucking close, his nerves too over-loaded, his chest thumping at what felt like hundreds of beats per minute, all for Zeph.

"Zeph…! Fuck, I—Zeph!" River didn't even try to keep his voice down, the last word slipping out in a rough growl of *I can't stop myself please, please…*

Zeph pulled him over the edge, driving deep into him while he tightened his grip around his shaft until River couldn't stop himself.

His chest burned, his eyes squeezed shut as he gasped for breath, all the tiny sounds of need and pleasure that spilled from his lips matched with grunts of approval and desire, the slapping of skin on skin, the creaking of the mattress…

His own mess splattered high up his own chest as he clenched tight around Zeph's throbbing erection, baring his teeth again. "*Yes!*"

And Zeph came undone in, around, over him, his weight pressing down against River's as he let go of River's cock and braced himself on the bed.

River snapped his eyes open so he could watch the animalistic pleasure etched on Zeph's face while those rough noises escaped his throat.

"River… I… *yeah…!*"

I what? River knew what Zeph had been about to say. *Exactly* what had nearly fallen from his lips, because as tough as Zeph was, as much as he walled himself off, River could read his face this very second, and it felt exactly like what was in his own heart.

But he stayed quiet and rubbed Zeph's back, pulled him close as Zeph's hips shuddered in desperate last erratic thrusts, spilling his passion deep within River's body.

When Zeph finally pulled back, they collapsed together, barely bothering to move except to pull the blanket over them. Their limbs stayed tangled the whole time, their cooling bodies still pressed together.

River needed Zeph as close as he could get him for one last night.

CHAPTER
Twenty-Two
RIVER

Mountains punched the landscape up on the drive back to L.A., young and raw and still rough-edged. River's eyes followed the changes in the landscape as cacti gave way to shrubs and mountains, and then softened again once they passed through the heart of the hills.

The mood between them was not like their flirtatious mood on the way there. Now, they chatted now and then about little things, but there was no mention of where they'd been or where they were going. Just the weather, the kinds of plants they passed, what fights were coming up for Zeph's friends, the awesome makeup palette River was going to buy with his winnings.

It was obvious they were both more introspective, but River didn't want to push his luck by making Zeph talk if he was in another of those moods.

Still, his heart jolted with disappointment stronger than he usually felt at the end of a trip when his apartment building came into view.

"There we go, then," Zeph said, stopping the car at the

curb. He got out, probably to help River get his suitcase and duffel bag.

Jesus. It felt like a lifetime ago he'd been waiting on the curb to be picked up, excited and nervous and unsure what to expect with this man he hadn't seen in so many years.

River drew on that memory, and how fucking *happy* he'd felt in this week and a half, to give him strength. Once the suitcases were out, his words rushed out. "We should talk about this."

"About...?" Zeph regarded him warily, clearly knowing where he was going.

"Us."

Zeph rubbed his face and shifted from foot to foot, then nodded. "Right. You mean the deal."

"Yeah. About that." This was like watching nail polish dry. River hurried the conversation along to the important part. "I want to continue it." Before Zeph could interrupt, he held up a hand. "I don't want to put pressure on you, but... I want more. More of what we had, and maybe more, you know, commitment. We'd have to see how it went. But I know I don't want it to end after ten days just because some calendar tells us it should."

"The deal," Zeph repeated softly, under his breath, as if reminding himself what this was all about.

"The deal," River echoed. Shit, Zeph probably needed a lot more time to process this if he hadn't been thinking about this proposal all the way from Vegas. "I don't want to pressure you, but... I know I'm not wrong. You felt it, too."

"Felt what?"

River scoffed at Zeph and folded his arms. He wasn't going to spell it out and scare Zeph out.

Maybe that was the wrong tack. Zeph was already

shaking his head, pulling his t-shirt down and shoving his hands into his pockets. "Yeah, no. You knew—we both knew—it was a limited-time thing."

"It *was*. It started that way. No law says it has to keep being that," River argued, trying to keep his voice down and appeal to Zeph's heart. "Not if we want more."

"I don't." Zeph wouldn't meet his eyes. He was looking at River's luggage. River raised one brow, tapped his foot, and waited for Zeph to make eye contact. When he didn't, River snapped his fingers.

"I don't believe you. Look me in the eyes and tell me that."

Zeph gritted his jaw, the muscle in his arms twitching as he pulled his hands out of his pockets and folded his arms instead. He did look at River, but his face was carefully neutral. Like he was in the ring, trying not to give any hints to the other fighter. "I don't want to extend the deal."

"Bullshit," River scoffed. "I like you. Time didn't change that. You've got some kind of feelings for me."

"I don't have *feelings* for you." Zeph wasn't looking at him again.

Whatever it was, it wasn't about River. He could tell when he was hitting a wall that was a lot older and more stubborn than their history. It pissed him off that there was nothing he could do to crack it from the other side.

"Zeph…"

But Zeph turned for the driver's side door, pulling it open. "I better get home before traffic gets bad."

River managed to hold back his tears. He raised a hand quickly. "Right. See you."

He got something like a *see you* back from Zeph in some manly grunt, but he didn't wait around. He listened to Zeph pull away as he hauled his luggage to the front door of the building.

River managed to wait until the cold walls of his apartment surrounded him again, and then he cried.

It wasn't easy feeling the pain of rejection and knowing that he'd done just that to pretty much every guy who'd tried to turn a hookup into more. Every fucking time one of them tried to tell *him* they felt a chance for more, he hadn't felt it himself. It felt a bit like nasty karmic payback.

But it was ten times worse knowing that Zeph, whether he knew it or not, wasn't in that boat. They both felt whatever crazy fucking chemistry pulled them together like magnets after five years without a word from each other.

We could be so good together, if he'd give us a chance.

Twenty-Three

RIVER

Normally at this time on a Friday night, River would be trading drinks for kisses, and then mutual fondling on the dance floor. He could sometimes get his hand into the other guy's pants before Kev, the glass collector, elbowed him on the way past to tell him to take it to the bathroom.

But for once, he wasn't keen to go out. Not even to the low-key bar around the corner where he could watch TV with the usual crowd of cuddly bears there who'd adopted him as a mascot. They loved to buy him drinks to hear his stories of what he'd done lately, and they always had a way of cheering him up.

Fuck, not even going out with Kyle to dance as badly as they could at a straight club and draw everyone's attention.

It was only supposed to be a fling, but he hadn't expected it to be... well, so much like a breakup. It felt like one, which as far as he was concerned gave him a free pass for a pizza, ice cream, and beer night. Screw leaving the house.

He'd only cried for a few minutes and felt sorry for

himself for a few more before he hit the shower, changed into sweatpants and a t-shirt, and unpacked.

Grumbling to himself the whole time about men with fucking emotional brick walls, he settled on a pizza order and then phoned it in. Then, he cleaned the living room a little and made a blanket nest for himself on the couch in front of the TV.

Kyle texted before long.

Made it home? Or will I have to send a search party??

River cracked a quiet smile.

Yeah thanks babe, he added a kissing emoji. *Had a good week?*

Quiet without you around.

Hey, I think that's an insult... River snorted.

Kyle sent a winking face, then the running man emoji.

River smiled to himself, tapping his phone on his knee. No, texts weren't the right place to fill Kyle in. Besides, everything was still too raw for him—the stalker, Zeph's clear feelings for him and denial of them…

God, now that he was waiting for pizza, he was actually starving. It was supposed to arrive any minute now.

He texted back, *Shows went great. Made lots of $. Getting that kit.*

Yay! Nic says: woot!

River smiled and rolled his eyes.

Yeah yeah, lovebirds. Get a room. Pizza's here!

He shoved his phone in his pocket and hurried for the door when he heard the buzzer, pressing the button to let the delivery guy in without picking up the phone. He tapped his foot, waiting the minute or so it took them to climb the stairs to his apartment.

There was the knock on the door.

River grinned as he pulled it open, and then he froze.

That… wasn't a delivery guy. No baseball hat and polo shirt, no pizza in his arms.

But he knew the guy's face.

It hit him at the exact same second the guy started toward him, jamming his foot in the door.

"You!" River gasped, grabbing the knob to keep the door only half-open.

The asshole at the bar he'd nearly fought with.

Wait. The bar in *Vegas*. Which meant only one thing: this was his stalker.

"Let me in, baby. Let me treat you like you deserve." The creep's words distracted him from the punch to his stomach until it was too late. He tried to shove his body through the door, crowding up close to River, his breath hot and hands wandering toward River's hip and chest.

Winded but not down, River growled and stomped on the guy's foot. "Fuck *off.*"

It only seemed to amuse the bigger man. His eyes were dark with some kind of fucked-up desire River didn't want to see within a hundred miles of him. "Tell me that when I have you tied down—"

This time, River was ready for the hits. He ducked and took one to the shoulder, using his own foot to jam the door half-closed while he aimed a right-hook through the door and bit the guy's arm when he tried to shove River backward.

For the first time, the guy's confidence faltered, but he still leered as he stumbled. "Feisty little minx." He licked his lips. "Just like the night we met, remember?"

"*Out!*" River landed a knee squarely in the guy's groin and shoved him back.

The guy grunted, but managed to get in another comment. "You're... gonna... kiss that better."

River slammed the door shut with his hip. He slid both locks into place, but it didn't feel like enough. Nothing felt like enough. Burning down the apartment and moving to the other coast, *maybe*. Or Thailand.

He took a few steps back from the door toward the kitchen while he grabbed his phone from his pocket and called the cops. He grabbed a knife and waited in the hall a few paces back as the guy tried the doorknob, and then went suspiciously quiet outside the door.

Fuck, fuck, fuck.

Zeph was right, and he'd never know. He'd picked up a stalker. All he could do was call 911 and hope *these* cops cared.

CHAPTER
Twenty~Four
ZEPH

Facebook was the modern equivalent of a masquerade.

Zeph didn't know a lot about that kind of history, but he imagined people put on facades about how well their merchanting or piracy businesses had gone while they looked prettier than usual with powdered lead and slowly killed themselves.

Exactly like Facebook: people carefully constructing images of their perfect lives, perfect relationships, perfect jobs, perfect looks. In reality, it was the people who weren't on Facebook—the celebrities and bodybuilders and super-star charity volunteers and whatever—who got all the praise.

A lot of athletes shared his point of view, either because they were naturally more outdoorsy and active, or because they'd deliberately cultivated a single-minded focus on their own particular discipline.

That wasn't to say Zeph never used Facebook himself. He'd shared his account name with some of the queens that week. But he usually browsed without commenting, if he was on there at all.

Especially now that he had... well, some reason to avoid the damn site.

But his feed didn't have anything from River, so he relaxed as he scrolled down it, a beer in his hand. Until he hit the posts: Glam, RB, and a lot of names he didn't recognize commenting on a post by Tina about River. The top reaction type was *sad*.

His heart jolted with fear for a second as he skimmed it.

For those of you who know River, word's already spread that he was attacked yesterday. That rumor is true but he wanted me to tell you all he's fine.

The comments were horrified, shocked, seeking details or offering solidarity. But there were no more details about what exactly had happened.

Fuck. Last night, after he'd dropped River off? What the fuck had happened in those few hours? He could only assume it was some homophobic dimwit, but maybe it was worse. An ex? Another stalker? Surely to God not the *same* stalker?

Zeph's grip on his bottle was so tight his knuckles were white. He took a breath and acknowledged the thought at last: if he'd agreed to continue with their... deal, affair, whatever you wanted to call it... would River not have been hurt? Maybe he'd been out getting some and hit on the wrong guy. Maybe, maybe, a hundred *maybes*, and he'd never get an answer.

Just like Anton. If he'd been around that night, maybe that car crash never would have happened. He'd kicked himself endlessly since then over the years, wishing he'd been a little more attentive, a little more thoughtful.

This was his chance to make up for it. It wasn't just his attraction to River, on whatever the hell level that existed—

as friends, or the forbidden allure of exes, or the new feelings River had brought up in him. It was repentance.

Zephyr North, of all people, seeking repentance. It hurt to smile about, but he did anyway.

Fuck, there was no good way out of this. Zeph closed his laptop and rubbed his temples as he set his beer aside, untouched but for the first couple gulps. He tried to think through his options.

If Zeph showed up, it would look like he was trying to get close out of pity to soothe his ego after the sting of rejection. But he didn't want River to go through all of this—first the Vegas stalker, now whatever the fuck this had been—alone.

Nobody deserved to be alone, least of all River, and at the same time, nobody was more likely to push everyone else away and insist on taking the brunt of it by himself.

That was stupid. Zeph was fully capable of protecting River, but if he didn't want his help…

Oh. That was it. Zeph sat up straight, catching his breath as the plan formed.

He could teach River self-defense. Not just street fighting, the kind that got him out of dive bars safely, but the kind that would help him flip an attacker over his shoulder and serve him his balls on a platter.

And if they wound up sharing more like they had over the last couple weeks… Zeph rubbed his chin as he pushed himself to his feet, trying not to let any specific memories distract him and necessitate a detour to the bathroom.

Well, he wouldn't turn River down a second time.

And after what had happened to Anton, he wasn't going to make the same mistake. It was up to River to accept help, but he was going to be there and make the offer.

Just as long as River didn't take it the wrong way.

Twenty-Five

RIVER

"HE SAID HE DOESN'T FEEL ANYTHING FOR YOU? ASSHOLE," Kyle scoffed.

"Right," RB agreed instantly, leaning in from the other side of the sofa. "You'd tell us the same if someone said that to us. You *have* in the past."

River resisted the urge to defend Zeph. The instinct prickled inside his brain, his gut, his very fingers and toes. He wanted to jump to Zeph's defense and explain it away, but Kyle and RB weren't going to let him do that.

It hurt to be forced to admit that Zeph had hurt him, but that sting of rejection was nothing compared to the rest of it.

"So I moped around and ordered pizza for myself, and when it came... it wasn't the pizza. It was the stalker. He tried to shove his way inside, he hit me... he said creepy shit, like I said... but I kicked him out and called the cops."

"Fuck," Kyle hissed. "You could have told us about him. We could keep you company."

River shook his head. "No, I'll be fine. It didn't shake me

that much," he fibbed. "Cops said they're looking for footage and took a description and everything. They're taking it a little more seriously than the Vegas one, at least. And he said he'll call the guys in Vegas and see what they've turned up there."

"If anything," RB muttered.

River was inclined to agree. He was sure hell would freeze over before they'd do anything about a stalker without a physical attack to investigate, and maybe even after that. Still, he shrugged. "Worth a try. Someone has to know the guy. Oh, Jesus. The creepiest part… while I called the cops he was all quiet outside, and I looked out but I couldn't really see anything, it was weird. I figured he was covering the peephole."

The other two were holding their breath, waiting on him.

River's gaze strayed to the door, where the hole was covered with tape and cardboard now. He was figuring out how to add metal to that. "But he'd… unscrewed the peephole to look through."

"You're fucking kidding me," Kyle hissed. "Jesus *Christ*."

"Yeah. Hopefully the cops got fingerprints from the door or something, at least." River drew a breath, about to explain how the report had gone, when there was a knock on the door.

He flinched without meaning to, then winced. That wouldn't exactly persuade either of his friends that he wasn't torn up about it.

Kyle eyed him as he stood, clearly choosing not to address it at that moment. "I'll get it."

River couldn't argue that. He just watched, fingers curled tightly with nerves, until the door opened.

Unmistakable even from a distance, Zeph's broad frame filled the doorway.

River's first instinct was joy, and then he remembered. The moment his heart sank was… crushing in itself. Now he wasn't just sad about the not-breakup, but about the split-second where Zeph's arrival had meant…

What? Safety? Warmth? Love?

Shit.

"Now isn't a good time," Kyle began.

River pushed himself to his feet to interrupt his friend, against his better instinct. Maybe having Zeph there would make him feel like it would have days ago, if only for a few minutes. "No, come in."

Even from behind, River could read Kyle's body language. His best friend stayed in the doorway just long enough to make it clear he wasn't happy Zeph was coming in, and he'd sooner see him leave, before stepping back and holding the door open for him.

Zeph thanked him in a murmur, and River followed Zeph's gaze to RB.

His other best friend had his arms folded coolly as he nodded to acknowledge Zeph.

Oh, shit, they're giving him the bad cop, bad cop treatment.

River's lips twitched slightly. He couldn't say part of him wasn't pleased about that.

"What are you doing here?" River asked, meeting Zeph as Kyle brushed past him to sit down. They stood near the kitchen table, River fidgeting with the zipper on his sweater.

"Uh, I heard about what happened," Zeph waved a hand toward River, and River recognized the up-and-down sweep of a man looking him over for injuries. "I… shouldn't have phrased things the way I did yesterday. I care about you, and, uh, I wanna help out."

River was shocked enough for a moment to be rooted to the spot. For Zeph, saying that in words and not actions was basically a wedding vow... or an apology.

"How? The guy's gone," River shook his head. "And he probably won't try again knowing the cops are involved. Not the same way, at least."

"Yeah, but he could follow you anywhere," Zeph stressed, leaning forward. "I can teach you self-defense. Not that you don't know some, but... properly. The techniques the pros use."

River recoiled. This was going south from the apology Zeph had been seemingly offering moments ago. He sure as fuck didn't want Zeph's pity, or being taken care of like he couldn't handle himself. "No. I don't need help."

Zeph opened his mouth, then sighed. "Don't do that—"

"I took care of myself yesterday." River walked toward Zeph, and just as he'd thought, Zeph didn't hold his ground. He backed down, not letting River break his personal space bubble.

And that was exactly what River had expected, too. He especially didn't want to be taken care of by Zeph, of all people, when... it was totally irrational post-not-breakup hormones, but River wanted all or nothing.

Zeph had rejected *all*, and River had spent the last day coming to terms with that.

"It's a standing offer." Zeph took the hint, though, and strolled for the door, letting River see him out.

"It can stand somewhere else."

"River—"

"Thanks for checking in on me. He didn't hurt me," River

told Zeph firmly. "I kicked him out. The cops are identifying him. It's over."

It sure as fuck *was* over, in every sense. River didn't need anyone. In the back of his mind, River knew damn well he wasn't trying to convince others yet.

He had to start by convincing himself.

CHAPTER
Twenty~Six

RIVER

RIVER *KNEW* WHAT THE FUCK HE WAS DOING. HE KNEW THE store, he knew his new coworkers, he knew the product line. But first-day nerves were never easy, and mentally, a small part of him was still in Vegas. After such a long vacation there, no wonder.

"Since you know your stuff already, and you've gone over the training materials… you can work the floor for your first day, get familiar with the product line and some of our regular customers."

His new boss at the makeup store was nice, at least. Ashley treated him like the other associates, not some rare unicorn to be fawned over or, worse, a less likeable oddity.

He let the other associates have the first few customers who approached, waiting until they were busy before he took his own first customer.

"Welcome. Can I help you find anything?"

The customer turned him down, so River told her he'd be there if she needed anything, then kept his distance to watch her browse and see what he could suggest.

It wasn't anything he hadn't done at the larger department stores, but this time, it was all one brand. That made his job a little easier, because he didn't have to sell people on its benefits or try to mix and match recommendations from different counters.

By noon, he'd settled into the routine, and when he came back from lunch, he rolled into the second part of his shift feeling confident and in his element.

This was what he loved to do, and he loved every second of it. He'd already helped someone choose a makeover, talked about new eyeshadow palettes with a few friends shopping together, and helped a few of his coworkers find products.

Now, he had a university-aged group of women talking about lipsticks.

"Mattes would actually look great on your complexion," he assured one of them. "The key is just getting the right color. I bet that's what went wrong before."

"See? I told you," another one said.

"Like what?"

This was the best bit—the educated guess, the trial and error, until he found just the right shade that made her light up when he showed her her own reflection.

The first two looked good on her but didn't pique her interest. He chose a shade of pink with a little more fuchsia, pretty confident this one would do the trick.

As he turned from the lipstick rack to the makeup chair again, he saw someone out of the corner of his eye.

Short, stocky, close-cropped hair. Alarm bells went off, and his heart jolted in his chest.

River turned for a better look, his shoulders rising.

Fuck. Thank God. Not his stalker.

He tried to shrug it off, focusing his attention on the

young woman who was supposed to be in the spotlight. He had the advantage of being able to chat freely with them and let them flirt with him in good fun. If he wasn't careful, he'd end up picking up a bunch of new girl friends here.

River tried to bend his thoughts that direction as he shared a laugh with them over the yellow shade another had found, then explained the kind of dramatic look he'd create with it while layering fuchsia onto his Q-tip.

But his mind was still on that split-second where he'd seen his stalker instead of some ordinary guy lingering outside the makeup store. That happened a hundred times a day—his nerves couldn't afford to think every bored husband or friend was a stalker.

He was just being jumpy. He'd settle, given time.

But he hated that Zeph was right, even in small part. And he hated that a tiny part of him had expected Zeph to be there, watchful and alert. And that same tiny, traitorous part of him wished he hadn't shoved Zeph out so fast yesterday.

River's heart hurt too much to appreciate making his first sale at this new job.

CHAPTER
Twenty-Seven

RIVER

WOODY'S WAS MORE OF A HOME TO RIVER THAN HIS OWN apartment, even with its cute artwork and comfy couch. A little style had nothing on the plain place with such a big heart.

He felt it every time he walked into Woody's—and other gay bars, too, but most of his loyalty lay here.

Coming here meant potential friends and fucks and both in one. It meant safety, not having to worry that hitting on the wrong guy would land you dead in an alley later. It meant the joy of moving your body to music, at the same moment as a hundred others did in their own rhythm and style.

It meant the solidarity of looking around, knowing that if everyone here hadn't gone through exactly the same shit, they'd at least had *some* shit happen to them. It was easy to tell who'd just had a bad day, and nobody had to say a word about it—but some people would listen, too, even to a total stranger.

Hell, it meant being able to wear whatever he wanted and

know exactly the responses he'd get. Even if some of these muscled bros looked down on him for it, they weren't going to do more than make some catty comment like they hadn't once been skinny, badly-dressed, and eager to please.

It was the closest thing to a church River had ever experienced or ever wanted to. His love for the place, for the stall everyone had an unspoken agreement was for blowjobs, for the damn sticky dance floor and the cracked mirror that made it hard to reapply lipstick and the initials carved under the bar top, swelled so fiercely in his chest that he had to blink back tears.

People came here to love and be loved on days when they had nothing and the world had chipped away at both, and they came here to celebrate and draw out the end of great days.

Today had been one of those great days for him. His first day on the job couldn't have gone better, apart from his own jumpiness.

But mostly, he was looking for someone to distract him, because as the day went on, he wished more and more that he could text Zeph about his day. Zeph would have laughed about him dropping knowledge on one stuck-up customer until she apologized for not taking him seriously.

That Vegas trip hadn't been fucking long enough, and at the same time, it had been a little too long. Maybe if they'd done a deal for a week, or a few days, they could have walked out with their hearts intact.

Instead, here he was at the bar, sipping his rum and Coke and looking around at the faces—many more familiar than his own long-forgotten relatives and others new.

He could have curled up with Zeph in front of the TV while he talked about his day before they had great sex and fell asleep together, curled up, listening to each other's breathing even out and slow down.

As he kept reminding himself: oh, well. That ship had sailed without them on board. He had to make the best of it.

But it was pretty hard to make the best of it with Zeph standing right there, wearing that half-smile that had first drawn him to the tall, broad man like a moth to a fucking candle.

Zeph had singed River's wings, and he still couldn't help picking his way through the crowd until he reached the part of the bar where Zeph leaned.

"Fancy meeting you here."

Zeph visibly brightened when he heard River, turning to take him in. "Oh. Come here often?"

"Not often enough." The innuendo was too fucking hard to resist, even if it was the last thing River should have been doing.

"I'm sure we can fix that."

"Hard to fix some things," River answered.

"Easy to get hard sometimes," Zeph countered.

"But it's hard being easy." River raised a brow. "Taking tips from my stalker?"

Zeph's expression flickered for a moment, but then he grinned and took it in stride. "Fair enough. But you approached me."

"I…" River blushed. Fucking fair enough, indeed. "Yeah." He tipped back his glass and drained the rest of the liquid, then pushed it over the bar. Jesus, he hadn't had nearly enough for this conversation.

Zeph eyed him. "I'd offer to buy you another, but I don't think you want anything from me."

"There's one or two things," River muttered, eyeing him. He could take that however he wanted.

Zeph drained his beer and set it aside. "Oh?"

"Use your imagination." *It's fertile, to say the least.* Half the creative sex they'd had came from Zeph's ideas.

Zeph's eyes darkened for a moment as he glanced River up and down. "I thought you didn't want me doing that, either."

"I never said that." River itched to tip back another shot or two and do something dumb, but if he was going to do something stupid, he wanted to do it more-or-less sober.

"Anything for you lovebirds?" It was Austin, the other bartender. He hadn't been privy to River's melancholy mood on the other side of the bar, and they *were* standing about close enough to be boyfriends, practically whispering in each other's ears.

Still, being mistaken for a couple *now*? It itched. It was time for him to go home. He was tired anyway, and clearly not getting laid tonight.

River shook his head at Austin, then turned from the bar and headed for the door. Zeph followed, and he'd expected no less. And the wicked part of him he was starting to hate was glad.

He was strong enough to say no to Zeph, but not strong enough to ask for him.

CHAPTER
Twenty~Eight

ZEPH

A LIFETIME OF BEING FUCKED-UP DIDN'T GO AWAY BECAUSE
one gorgeous, sweet, perfect guy looked at him the right way
and asked for permission to care about him.

Zeph knew he was fucked up. He always had been. But
there was no way in hell he was going to fuck River up, too.
He'd screwed up, and he had to at least set things right.

Let River know that it wasn't his fault, that he'd been this
kind of man for a lot longer than he'd known River, even if
this was his second time around with him.

"River?" Zeph stopped at the curb when they were
outside and safely out of earshot of the bouncers. When his
lover—ex-lover—ex-boyfriend… whatever the hell River was
to him… turned to him, he cleared his throat. "Can we go
somewhere quiet?"

River didn't shoot him down like he feared. Instead, he
eyed him for a moment. "Why?"

"I owe you an explanation for… everything."

River's shoulders slumped, and all Zeph wanted to do
was pull him into his chest and hug him until that beautiful

smile was back. It hurt Zeph deeper than he'd imagined to know that *he* was the source of that pain.

"Yeah. Okay," River sighed, nodding down the street. "Come back to my place, then."

They walked quietly. To take his mind off the thrum under his skin that he couldn't decipher, Zeph glanced around and admired the details. The evening was cool but not crisp, and clear enough to see a few stars. Here on the outskirts of L.A., that was rare.

And he was walking beside the only guy whose name had been on his lips when he'd woken up in the morning without having spent the night next to him.

Out of the blue, River's name had been the first thing in his head.

Fucking weird.

When they reached River's place, Zeph didn't waste time heading for the couch, arranging his hands in his lap while River brought them glasses of water.

River crashed on the couch next to him, keeping a good foot or two away—the distance normal friends would. But Zeph knew that for River, that was practically a world away.

"So, shoot." River was the first to break the silence, and he kept it simple.

Zeph cleared his throat, suddenly realizing that he knew what he wanted to say, but not how. And it was the *how* that usually made the difference, as their last encounter had proven.

River had taken his offer of help exactly the way he didn't want him to, and he didn't know how to keep that from happening again.

But he had to try.

"I turned you down really hard the other night. I'm sorry.

I didn't mean to, um… be that blunt. And you're right that I feel… things… for you. Obviously. Like I said yesterday about caring about you."

River was still watching him, his brow quirked slightly, so Zeph hadn't totally fucked up yet. He drew a breath and went on.

"But I don't do relationships."

River propped his chin on his fist, his elbow on the back of the couch. It felt like he was indulging Zeph for a moment as he half-smiled and drawled, "Me neither."

But he didn't know half the truth of it. Shit. That meant Zeph had to tell him. He didn't tell people this—he had no idea how to start.

Zeph drew a quick breath and shook his head. "No. I mean, I can't. Because everyone close to me gets hurt, or… worse."

River went still, the smile vanishing from his lips, but he gave Zeph the gift he most needed right now—silence and attentiveness, not interruptions. The space was almost enough for Zeph to get his thoughts in order.

"I… You know my name? Zephyr, right? It's why I chose it. In mythology, Zephyr kills the people he loves. Maybe not on purpose, but bad things just… happen. Around me, too. My parents died, you know that. My best friend… you never —I never said." Zeph tried to keep his voice level, but it cracked. "Anton. He picked up a crazy stalker. Crashed his car trying to escape him. I can't… keep… people around."

River was pale now, his lips parting as he pulled his head away from his fist and sat up straighter. Zeph could hear the platitudes now, the apologies, the… pity. Shit. For a second, he felt like River had yesterday.

Zeph shook his head quickly. "And I've… I've been hurt,

too," he managed. He felt sick. His heart pounded worse than when he stepped out of the cage. He wanted to run—every instinct in his body told him to, and holding himself rigid on the couch was the best he could do.

He'd never come close to telling anyone this. Not since *then*, not since *them*.

River finally whispered, "I'm sorry. Not sorry for you, but sorry about what's happened to you."

Zeph looked away quickly to make sure his composure was still intact enough to handle this, then back at River and nodded, doing a weird little half-shrug thing that was supposed to tell River not to worry about it. Preferably to pretend he'd never said it.

"But, baby, you're not the only one who's been hurt."

The words rang in Zeph's ears for a moment. Did he mean...? The fury that laced his every breath scared even him for a second, and he'd spent a lifetime thinking of painful ways to end any man who got too close to him.

"Someone hurt you? I'll fucking kill them," Zeph whispered. His hand hurt, and he realized it was his nails digging into his palm.

River half-smiled. "Not the way I think you mean, but I understand pain. I don't have a family either, you know. It took me a long fucking time to find one best friend, let alone two, who *get* me. I can't find a man who sees past the lipstick and thinks of me as a real person with a heart *and* a brain, not just... an easy-access tight ass desperate for his manly dick. I understand pain, even if it's not the same kind. But you're an idiot."

Zeph hadn't pictured River responding *this* way. His jaw dropped, and all he could do was stare for a moment. "What...?"

"You're an idiot if you think that makes it okay to shut yourself off from the world. It hurts to love people, or to care about them, or to want to see where things go with them."

Zeph still couldn't breathe. "But I…" He didn't know how to put it into words: his animal brain told him to get out, flee, now. Another part of his brain just wanted to touch River and hold him, let those walls crumble at last.

But, shit, River didn't understand what a raw nerve he was touching… how dark Zeph's thoughts had gotten for those few seconds. How much he'd *meant it* when he said he'd kill any man who'd made River feel… well, feel like he did.

Impossible to love.

River was smiling slightly. "Your protectiveness there was sweet, though. Still saying you don't have feelings for me?"

Zeph had literally no other way out of this, so he chose the only way he could see: he rose to his feet and headed for the door. "I gotta get home. Thanks. Bye."

He wasn't sure which words he'd chosen for a few moments, just hoping he hadn't gone with *have a nice day* or *how have you been* or any other automatic phrase.

Before he knew it, he was jogging toward his apartment, his thighs burning, his lungs burning, his eyes burning.

The sidewalk was even, which was a mercy if he'd ever experienced one, because he couldn't slow down. Couldn't stop. Couldn't go back.

Not tonight.

CHAPTER
Twenty-Nine

ZEPH

GODDAMMIT, THIS WAS EASY.

To be fair, sparring with Tristan wasn't like sparring with a total newbie, but it also wasn't the challenge Zeph needed right now. He wanted to get his mind off all this shit.

They were taking the match casually as always, although they didn't get to spar often. Tristan couldn't afford bruises, in case he got an audition. But it was a great release for them both when they did get to do it.

Zeph circled Tristan once more, then stepped in to give him an opening. When Tristan took it, he faked leaning away until Tristan stopped his punch too soon, then leaned in for a couple of quick hits on the chest.

It would bruise his ego more than his body, and maybe make the lesson stick. He loved Tris, but the man never learned.

"Jesus," Tristan muttered under his breath while Zeph grinned. "Anyway, you were saying? He didn't like the self-defense idea."

"Right. So I went to Woody's and saw him the next night.

We talked, flirted a bit, and then the bartender... I guess he thought we were a couple, which scared him off."

He got another glancing blow off Tristan's shoulder and Tristan winced, then reciprocated with a well-placed kick.

The pain cleared Zeph's head. "Followed him out," he continued, backing off to catch his breath. Tristan made the right call by following, keeping close to him and forcing him against a wall. "Asked if I could come home and explain things."

His blows landed harder now, trying to get some space, but Tristan flipped him to the mat.

"I let you do that," he told his friend.

"Sure." Tristan straddled him, dodging his punch for the chin. "And?"

"And I went home, we talked. Told him my track record with friends and family and whatever."

He'd never *told* Tristan, but somehow the man knew. He'd brought up Zeph not having a family before, and Zeph had maybe helped him a little too well when he'd prepared for an audition for a character who'd just lost a friend in a sudden death.

He flipped Tristan and went for a chokehold, but Tristan wormed free and grinned infuriatingly. "And?"

"And he said I'm not the only one who's had it rough, blah blah, turned down my apology. I think."

"But did you actually say sorry?" Tristan rolled his eyes as he bounced to his feet again. It was like a red rag to a bull, and Zeph closed the distance between them with a few strides before landing a hard hit to his side.

"Yes, actually." Tristan nearly doubled over as Zeph managed a solid hit in the ribs. "He wants... I don't fucking know." He followed it up with another hit on pure instinct.

"Jesus fuck! Knock it off."

"What?" Zeph took a few paces back and raised his hands.

"I'm not auditioning for a punching bag role here, asshole." Tristan glared at him as he straightened up again.

With a little distance between them, the fighting instinct ebbed, and Zeph's brain was clearer again. He wasn't thinking like Tristan was Rhino anymore, a man more than capable of knocking him out in his next real fight if he wasn't on guard every single second in the cage.

Zeph winced. "Shit. Sorry. I got caught up."

"I know." Tristan rubbed his side, then smiled ruefully. "And I let you distract me with your dumb ass."

"What?" Zeph scrunched his face, then went for a towel as he hopped down. His gym had a few other fighters training there, too, but it was empty this time of night. They could talk and spar, and they were rarely interrupted. "Are you calling me a dumbass over the River stuff?" He chugged water and slumped against the cage to rest.

"Uh, *yeah*," Tristan grabbed his own water bottle and dumped half of it over his head, gasping with relief before he chugged the other half.

Zeph gave him a mildly offended look. He'd earned a few verbal lashings, but that was a little harsh. Sure, Tris didn't *know* about the… other thing… but he'd guessed by now after Zeph cut off a religion conversation. Tris hadn't brought up religion in years.

When Tristan was done drinking, he threw his empty bottle at Zeph, who automatically caught it after it bounced off his face.

"Hey," Zeph grunted.

"Just give a relationship a shot. Jesus, it's obvious. You want one."

Zeph grunted and threw back the empty water bottle as they walked over to the fountain. He shouldered in front of Tristan to refill his own first, so Tristan shoved him in the side first.

That meant they were good.

If only things with River were that easy.

Thirty

RIVER

IF EVERYTHING ELSE WENT WRONG, AT LEAST RIVER LOVED HIS new job. And today, he loved his friends more than usual, which was a tall order.

He looked up from studying the cash register behind the counter only to spot Dixie, whose nickname had become Delta after an embarrassingly well-known incident with an Air Force officer in the dark room, and Anna, who was the sweet young Andy. Neither of them were in drag, and they were heading straight for the store.

As they came in, he ducked out from behind the register to welcome them. "Hey, guys. What's up? I mean, how can I help you?"

"We heard about the new job and wanted to support you," Andy told him, grinning.

"And," Delta added, "maybe try the new eyeshadow range…"

"Ohhh my God," River gasped. "You haven't yet? It's incredible! It layers really well, *and* you can blend it for—oh my God, let me show you."

He was happy as anything to let them swatch the new shades on their skin, and when he got them into his makeup chair one at a time, showed them two of his favorite new looks with it.

Far from what a small part of him had feared, the sight of three guys clustered around the makeup counter didn't scare off the other customers. Instead, many of the women shopping as well as his own coworkers didn't bat an eye, and others were curious or amused.

Yeah, that was it. This job was officially cool.

"So we heard that a certain Zephyr showed up at your door," Andy teased. He was leaning on the counter while River worked on Delta, trying to persuade him to buy the full set since he knew Delta had the money for it and could seriously use some pro-grade stuff.

"Ugh, you bunch of gossips," River giggled. "Yeah."

"And?" Delta asked, peeking through one lid. River flicked his shoulder and he closed it again.

"And," River sighed, "he wanted to give me self-defense lessons, I'm sure they told you that, too."

"And they said you pretty much shoved him out the door again." When River cast him a startled glance, Andy pretended to zip his lips.

River couldn't blame them. Of course his relationship woes—if it could even be called that—were the talk of the scene. He so rarely had anything even resembling a relationship. Which was half the problem here, really, and the reason this hurt so much.

He distracted himself by standing back. "Mmhmm. So he showed up at the bar and apologized and explained he wasn't ready for a relationship and left, so, you know. Whatever." He stood back and waved a hand at Delta. "And?"

Andy whistled lowly. "I can't believe that blended together so well. How?" Being pretty new to the scene, Andy was still learning a lot from River, and he'd been watching the whole time. "Was that really because of the... makeup? Or is it the artist?"

"Little of this, little of that," River teased. "But you'll notice a lot better blending with the good stuff. It's not all brand name, though. I'm happy with everything from this brand—"

"Of course," Delta teased.

"Of course," River echoed, winking, "but other brands have some good lines and other really bad ones. They'll put out some limited-edition stuff that flakes right off your skin, or gets in your eyes, or doesn't blend with even their own stuff, let alone other people's."

"Oh," Andy murmured, then glanced at Delta. "So you're thinking of the full palette?" He glanced at the price tag on the display nearby and winced.

"You can start with a few base colors of the permanent line," River assured him. "Get four or six staple colors you use a lot. A few of these new ones are so flashy you'd only use them rarely."

"Or as your everyday grocery shopping shade, in your case," Delta teased, and River pretended to push his cheek away until he pushed him off the makeup stool. "Don't maul your customers! I'm going for the palette."

"You are?" River gasped teasingly as he plucked one off the display. "You'll love it."

"I already planned to buy it. I just wanted to see your spiel. You're very good at it," Delta winked.

River rolled his eyes at his friend. "Jerk. Away with you."

"No, but… back to Zeph," Andy pressed as he wiped the eyeshadow off with cleanser.

"What about him?"

"You gotta take those lessons. Maybe even try for more, because… I know I don't know you *that* well yet," Andy quickly added, "but you guys were great together, you know? You seemed really sweet on each other. But at the very least, he wants you to be safe."

"And if you don't get in touch, we will," Delta added, snatching the palette from him and flicking his chest. "So shape up."

River blinked at Delta now. "What?"

"Even if you don't want to learn it, we do," Andy told him as he picked out shades of eyeshadow to buy. "We've been talking about it. I mean, like, Glam's done some boxing… some of us did martial arts as kids or whatever… but it wouldn't hurt any of us to learn more."

River took them both up to the register so one of his coworkers could ring them in and credit him with the sale. "Maybe. Thanks for dropping by, guys."

"Thanks for the tips. I can't wait to play with this," Delta told him with a grin.

After they left, River turned more thoughtful, even as he moved from customer to customer and offered help.

Kyle and RB, despite giving Zeph the cold shoulder the other day, hadn't really commented on his decision to turn down the lessons. That made him suspect that they agreed with Delta and Andy.

And as much as he hated to admit it, River would be outmatched in a fair fight without the advantage of being in his doorway, and easily outmatched in an unfair fight. The creepy asshole had already shown that fair wasn't the way he played.

Maybe they were right, and he needed to learn to accept help. He'd done so for ten days in Vegas and, in the process, he'd stumbled on one of the best things he'd almost had.

It hurt to think about never being that close to Zeph again, but maybe this was Zeph's way of testing the waters between them, too. He seemed to want it as much as he didn't.

And River needed help. Just once in a while, he could let Zeph, of all people, help him.

CHAPTER
Thirty~One
RIVER

God help him, he was thinking about doing it.

River had been sitting on his couch with a now-cold cup of coffee in front of him for the last… half an hour? At least? His phone was pressed against his lips and between his palms, elbows braced on his knees.

He'd been thinking about calling Zeph that whole time, but he hadn't gotten up the courage to do it yet.

In thinking about it, though, all his friends were right, along with his own gut instinct. He had to ignore the impulse to cut Zephyr out of his life before he could get his heart broken, because it was too late for that.

Even if they weren't together, Zeph had always made him feel safe, and he needed that. He hated admitting it, but it was so fucking rare, and it soothed his soul in ways he didn't fully understand.

River clicked the button on top of his phone to glance at the time, then registered it.

Shit. He'd been delaying the call for too long, and now he really had to get to work, or he'd be late.

He launched into action, grabbing his keys on the way past the table and swaying into the bathroom just long enough to make sure he looked all right. Yeah—he could touch his lips up in the car before he headed into the mall.

After work, then, he'd call Zeph.

"River? Can you come into the office for a sec?"

That was Ashley's voice catching River on the way to the floor, just as he tightened the makeup artist's equivalent of a tool belt—the kit he wore around his waist.

"Of course." But instantly, River's mind was turning over the possibilities.

Maybe someone had complained about his drag queen friends coming in. Maybe he'd oversold or he wasn't selling enough. He'd forgotten what one of the shades looked like, but one of his coworkers had helped him. But everyone did that from time to time…

He stepped into the office, glancing around the space with its stark furnishings. Nothing detracted attention from the campaign posters, paint-swatch-like palettes, and celebrity photos plastering the walls.

River closed the door and dropped into the chair opposite Ashley, crossing his legs at the knee and folding his hands. "Yes?"

Ashley's lips were pressed together slightly as she pulled an envelope from her drawer.

It was in a faded flower card envelope, which made his heart sink instantly.

Shit, shit, *shit*. No way.

Half of him hoped that it was Zeph apologizing for

talking about his feelings and running, but then there'd be flowers accompanying it.

"Please tell me there wasn't some dead animal with that," River mumbled as he reached out to take the envelope. There was no name on it, but there was no question the card was for him.

Part-time lady, full-time whore. The more you tease, the harder it is. xox.

He tried not to touch the card as he slid it back into the envelope, but no way was there any fingerprint evidence left now.

No need to ask how she knew it was his, then.

"I need to know what's going on." Ashley's expression was sympathetic, if professional. "You're not the first staff member to have… an unwanted admirer."

"Oh, thank God. I didn't ask for this," River breathed out, relaxing into his chair as he covered his face with his hand for a moment to try to hide the extent of his relief.

The last thing he wanted was to be the new guy who was bringing attention with him.

"Have you gone to the cops yet?"

"Yeah. There's a detective assigned… I'll give this to him." he waved the envelope slightly, then pocketed it, avoiding her gaze. "He might be on the security tapes, huh?"

"It was kind of hidden under a display, so it could have shown up anytime in the last day or two," Ashley told him. "They can go through the mall security tapes but it might not yield much."

"Shit," River muttered, then winced. "Sorry."

Ashley shook her head. "Don't worry about it. How long has this been going on?"

"A couple weeks. Between the interview and my first day,

remember I said I was going on a tour? I managed to pick this creep up then." River realized how he'd phrased it and winced. "I mean, he picked *me*."

Ashley nodded. "And he's followed you to… home, too?"

"Yeah. Or he wouldn't know where to find me at work. Jesus, he's everywhere." River's gut clenched as he realized this was exactly what the guy wanted him to feel. And he didn't even know his name.

"Okay. Keep me posted on what the detective said. We can go to mall security, too, and make sure someone walks you to your car. At least let a coworker do that."

River shook his head. "I don't want any of the girls getting hurt on my account." He pushed his lip around with his teeth. Shit, he should be able to deal with this without dragging the whole world into… whatever the fuck made guys lose their minds about him and insert him into that world of fantasy.

"You're no different than them," Ashley said firmly, leaning in over the desk to catch his eyes. "You don't have to deal with this on your own. But if he's that creepy, we'll make sure mall security walks out with everyone who closes up, then."

River rubbed his face again, trying not to smear his makeup. "Thanks," he murmured. "It… shouldn't be long before they catch him, I hope. And I'm getting an MMA fighter friend to teach me self-defense, if he agrees, which… I think he will. I'm texting him right now," he laughed under his breath. Time to stop pretending he wasn't rattled.

"Okay. Keep me posted, River. I'll go grab someone from mall security right now."

River nodded and pulled out his phone as he stepped out

of the office, letting her pass. He leaned in the hall and composed a quick text.

Can we talk about self defense? I hate saying it but I need help. Please.

He ignored the shame that swept through him and burned his cheeks as he hit Send.

"Dress like that and you're asking for it."

River was seventeen, holding together the ripped-open front of his blouse. He'd just made it through the front door without the guys next door getting hold of him. And his dad had finally been home early enough to see. His lucky streak couldn't have lasted forever.

"Get that shit off."

Not even a dress or a skirt, but something tame. He hadn't been sure of it, but now he was. He was going to lose his family the moment he was eighteen, if not sooner.

So River backed down. He lied. He said what he had to in order to survive: that it was a dare by the guys at school.

A decade later, he'd barely remember what words his father used, but all of them hurt. His dad told him off for letting the guys treat him like a girl. If only they knew what he got up to during recess.

But when he couldn't keep it the secret they all pretended it was anymore, or when he was eighteen and he could get the fuck out—he honestly wasn't sure which would happen first—he was going to be damn well ready.

River pulled his mind off the memory and pocketed his phone. Ashley didn't mind if they used them on the floor, as long as customers weren't around.

Good thing, because waiting for Zeph's response otherwise would be a damn long day.

But, much sooner than he expected, it went off and he

had to dig it right back out again, his heart pounding until he read the answer.

Of course. When and where?

River closed his eyes for a second and thanked whatever God was out there for Zephyr North.

CHAPTER
Thirty-Two
RIVER

ZEPH'S HAND SLID ALONG RIVER'S STOMACH, UP TO HIS CHEST as his other arm locked around his neck. River leaned back into him without thinking twice, his heart thumping.

"No," Zeph's voice murmured, close to his ear. Warm breath tickled the hairs on the back of his neck. "Think."

Right. Shit. He was supposed to be fighting the bastard off. They were going through the scenario slowly a few times before taking it at full speed.

River turned his head, tucking his chin in the crook of Zeph's elbow, against his chest. Zeph had explained that this way, he couldn't lock his arm around River's throat for a chokehold, and his arm pressed against his collarbone instead.

Then, he grabbed Zeph's arm on either side of the elbow, pressing it into his own chest. He started to turn and Zeph shook him slightly.

"No. Think."

"I *am* thinking," he mumbled into Zeph's arm, then caught

his breath. Zeph's left arm around his neck, which meant he had to turn left. Sneaky asshole would do the opposite of what he'd done the first time.

And it was really hard to think with that muscled body pressed up behind him, the scent of Zeph filling his nose, the occasional brush of his cock against him when they were snuggled together—no, pressed together—just right.

The thought of it being his stalker instead was enough to chill him for long enough to think. He shifted his feet, turned the left foot out, and pressed the ball into the floor.

Ready for the spin. Just like dancing, only… more painful. And without a willing partner.

He pivoted on his ready left foot, his right leg half-circling around until he'd reversed his stance and then some, and he faced Zeph. All the while he kept his hold tight on Zeph's arm.

This was the important part. The hold was definitely broken, but he wasn't sure he got what Zeph had said he could do next.

"You can run, or…" Zeph prompted, leaning over to let him keep the hold on his arm.

"Or… Right!" He kept the hand that was closer to Zeph's shoulder firmly in place, then slid his other hand up to his wrist to pull that down while he pushed up on the elbow.

That was a move he'd naturally be inclined to try anyway when someone got a little too handsy—he'd had to before—but he'd never done it with this stance.

Zeph hit the floor and grunted, and River quickly let go as he hovered over him, half-crouching. "You okay?"

"Yep."

River bounced on the balls of the feet. "That was right, right?"

"Good. If I hadn't hit the ground, if I'd tried to hold on and grab you from behind with the other hand or hit you in the nuts, you could keep your body out of range and step to the side, keep your hands pushing and pulling to reverse my arm even further. Anatomy demands I'll fall sooner or later."

"Right. But I think you appreciate your rotator cuff."

"More than you know." Zeph grinned up at him as he pushed himself to his feet. "Good job."

The awkwardness of having Zeph's hands slide along his body, positioning him and guiding him through the moves, had started to fade. Now, instead of awkwardly arousing, it was just plain thrilling.

Which really wasn't helpful for learning anything, or for diffusing the tension between them.

"Once more, full speed," Zeph told him.

This time, River had a mental image of that creepazoid in his head and he was ready.

Zeph went in with his right arm this time, so River tucked his chin, turned right, broke the hold, and turned his arm up to dump him on his back.

"Yes!" Zeph hissed from the floor.

River gave him a hand to pull him to his feet, and for just a moment, it felt like they could be just buddies.

Just men wrestling around, practicing…

Shit, he hadn't let go of Zeph's hand, and he was swaying toward him. The sparks flew between them, and his cheeks were burning.

Zeph's hands slid along his hips to his sides, and he lost his momentary doubt that this was a test of his newly-acquired skills.

This was all their chemistry, once again unstoppable and hotter than even he could understand.

River's lips met Zeph's, and his weight draped along Zeph's body, and he was falling into Zeph, heart and mind and soul.

CHAPTER
Thirty~Three

ZEPH

Teaching River self-defense was more rewarding than training any newbie ever had been.

Not only did River learn fast once he had the reason behind the physical movements figured out, but he was confident. He'd fought before to keep himself safe, anyone with Zeph's experience could tell. He just needed help stringing the moves together in the best order.

That fact alone made Zeph's blood boil, but he didn't mention a word. Someday, if he were *very* lucky and managed to go that long without totally pissing River off and ending their friendship, River might tell him more. It wasn't hard to guess anyway.

The thrill of accomplishment surged through Zeph when he tried it full-speed and hit the ground, his arm giving a sharp twinge until he grunted for River to let go.

"Yes!" he exclaimed, beaming up at him.

River might be dressed in loose, comfortable clothes with no makeup, but he'd never looked prettier. Seeing him sweat and work out would never get old.

It had taken all Zeph's focus not to drag the loose t-shirt and sweatpants off his body and kiss him from head to toe until he begged for more.

When River grabbed his hand, their palms pressing alone made his skin tingle as he let him help him get to his feet. Fuck, he was going to need a minute before he got close to River again.

Or… not.

River's eyes were fixed on his, that gaze intense and as easy to read as ever.

Just when Zeph had wondered if they could tamp down the sparks between them that they were so desperately trying not to acknowledge, they ignited again.

River leaned into Zeph, and he couldn't stop himself. He needed to touch River, to kiss him, to hold him and make up for every damn thing he'd clumsily said to make River think he didn't want him.

He slid his hands from River's hips up his sides, under his shirt, and the bare skin had never felt better to touch.

They kissed hard, their bodies fitting together just right, River's lean thigh between Zeph's and his chest pressing against his. It was easy to support his weight, just as he had dozens of times before.

Zeph ran his hands slowly back down his back again, stopping just short of grabbing his ass.

Not that he didn't want to—he did, so badly it made his head spin—but he owed him words before he did that.

"I… should… hold on," he managed against those warm, sweet lips. He couldn't resist stealing a few more slow, deep kisses before he put his thoughts together.

"*I'm* holding on," River mumbled against his mouth, that devilish little smirk appearing.

Dammit. Every time he thought he had control of himself, River did something else that captivated him. Some tiny little mannerism he might not have even known would pull Zeph's interest straight back to him.

If MMA was his addiction, he'd never known one like it until River. He was fucking addicted to this man, too.

So much so that he'd nearly forgotten his training. They were close to his first fight—very close.

No sex until afterward.

It was, apparently, a distraction. Even if testosterone levels were elevated afterward, to get the benefits, he'd have to perform under the same conditions… Not that the idea of fucking River hard and fast in the dressing room before the fight didn't get Zeph hard on the spot, but *that* was better left to fantasy.

"What?" River whispered against his mouth, which brought his thoughts back to the moment.

Zeph slowly pulled back until River stood on his own two feet again, pushing a hand back through his hair as he chuckled. "Man, you kiss like nobody else." He ran a finger up the center of River's chest from around where he figured his belly button was to his collarbone.

"Compliment accepted, but tell me what's going through that brain of yours," River prompted, swatting his hand playfully.

"Oh. Right." *Jesus, focus for ten seconds. No wonder he doesn't want me fucking before a fight.* "Us," Zephyr murmured, clearing his throat.

He was pretty sure it was up to him to start that conversation, since he'd been the one to freak out and run the last time it was brought up.

River eyed him, then nodded slightly. "Mm?"

"You know why I'm so nervous about the idea, but... as long as I don't hurt you, I could... I would. I mean, I want to. I want *you*." Zeph was still having trouble with the actual words, but River, bless him, showed him more patience than he fucking deserved.

It actually made him... afraid? No, uneasy? Whatever the emotion, it hurt Zeph to be shown that much concern.

River's gaze was steady and knowing as he pulled his t-shirt back into place. "You've never hurt me."

"I..." Zeph furrowed his brows. "No?"

"Not once," River emphasized. "And I've never felt unsafe, or even unheard. You're the most considerate lover I've *ever* had."

"Oh." Zeph looked away to compose himself, and River looked away, too, to give him space. Again with the consideration. Zeph started to wonder if maybe River *could* make it work with him, despite his fucked-up brain.

"I'm not allowed to have sex until after the fight. That's in two days. Or... to hang out with you much," he admitted. "I had to practically bribe my trainer to get away. Bo would fucking rip into me five ways from Sunday if he knew what I was doing," he admitted with a laugh. He could see the look on Bo's face now. The risk of injury? Oh, yeah. He'd hear every conjugation of every swear word Bo knew, in every language.

Still, it was pretty funny. Maybe he'd tell Bo. In about a year, when he'd learned how to avoid the ear pinch Bo so loved when he was being an idiot. With his luck, he'd give him that same ear pinch when he heard about River, since everyone seemed to agree he needed to man up and give it a try with this guy.

Right. He had to say that. He could probably skip all the

rest of those words. "But I want to give it a try. I want you," Zeph repeated firmly.

And when River's cheeks rounded and he beamed at him like he'd been waiting a lifetime to hear those words, Zeph could read the answer on his face before he even spoke a word.

"You really want to try?" River sounded breathless, like he didn't know he deserved it. That, too, made Zeph want to pull him into his protective embrace until he could find and personally break the face of anyone who made him feel otherwise. "Yeah. If you do. I... yeah. I want you, Zeph."

Zeph breathed out slowly and looped his arms around his lover's waist, pulling him in to rest their foreheads together.

There was no manual to tell him how to handle a guy who made him feel things he'd never felt with any boyfriend or crush before. But he could deal with this, one step at a time.

Of course it was worth a try. More than that, even. It was worth all the weirdness and the uncertainty between them, and not knowing where exactly he stood.

River was worth his best fucking try.

CHAPTER

Thirty-Four

ZEPH

THE PRE-FIGHT ROUTINE WAS AS NATURAL AS BREATHING TO Zeph, but he'd never thought about how strange it looked to an outsider until now.

Cooking an extra portion of the protein-loaded light lunch for River, going for a quick jog with River by his side, heading to the gym for a warmup with River watching him and Bo...

It was *nice*.

Zeph was surprised at how damn well River fit in. He didn't distract them, but he watched closely as Zeph went through everything he and Bo had been practicing. The blend of wrestling, jiu-jitsu, Muay Thai, and kickboxing had been intense, because every discipline required different muscles. His goal of beating Rhino if they took it to the floor seemed achievable, but he and Bo were worried about what would happen if Rhino had been working on his upper-body strength and speed.

With the weigh-in over, he was eating as often as he could stand, and River didn't join in all the meals, but he also didn't look weirded out or tease him like he'd expected.

By lunchtime they were done training, not wanting to burn more energy than was totally necessary. With the adrenaline beginning to surge at the prospect of the fight that evening, it was hard for Zeph to keep his hands off River, but Bo took care of that by getting them both over to his place for a video-gaming marathon.

Kicking ass at Mario Kart had to help improve his morale, right? Next time, he'd have to train River in some of the warmup exercises he was doing so he could have another partner.

It startled Zeph how easily he thought of a *next time*. Thinking ahead to his next fight was something he strictly avoided until after a fight, so he had to squash that idea now. Even *after the fight* was dangerous.

His job now was to visualize the fight—every tiny detail from wrapping his hands to applying Vaseline, from walking up the stairs to the octagon to raising his hand in victory after the fight.

Once their gaming was done, River kept playing with Bo while Zeph walked around Bo's yard for a while, visualizing the trading of blows.

If Rhino *had* been working on upper body and had been using the BJJ reference to throw him off, he'd have to get the fight where he wanted it—on the mat.

That meant leg locks and grappling holds, using his weight to throw Rhino off-balance.

He closed his eyes, choosing a meditation pattern and breathing deeply as he walked the familiar circular gravel path around the birdbath.

He had to win this fight. All banter with Tristan about his

career prospects aside, he couldn't afford a losing streak now. And Rhino was a great guy, but dangerously good in the cage.

Once Rhino was down, he couldn't let him get back up.

"Is it time?" River looked anxious but excited as he sidled up to Zeph in the parking lot.

Bo was already waiting for him in the locker room. Zeph knew everything that was about to happen, right up until the first blow. From then on, it was down to a healthy mixture of skill and luck.

"Yep. I gotta go do my thing." Zeph didn't feel as nervous as he perhaps should have. "Are you staying?"

"Of course!" River assured him. "I'll be there to watch you win, babe."

A smile spread across Zeph's face as he gazed at River. As it turned out, hearing that felt like an extra confidence boost rather than an extra thing to feel nervous about. His worries on that front were laid to rest instantly.

Yeah, maybe this can work out.

"Okay. Cool. I'll see you after the post-fight medical," Zeph told River to give him an idea what to expect.

River nodded once, firmly, and then leaned in. He cupped Zeph's cheeks in his palms and pressed their lips together once. "Go kick his ass."

Zeph beamed at River and pulled back, then clapped his shoulder. "I will."

When he got to the locker room, Rhino was waiting to say hello. They half-hugged and clapped each other's backs as they joined the rest of the fighters who were up tonight.

They were going third in the lineup, right after what promised to be a hell of a fight between an upstart newbie and one of the older, more experienced guys in the sport. Zeph just hoped they could hold the audience's interest after that.

One of the other fighters, Odin, waved to catch his attention. "You showed up."

"Wouldn't miss a chance to beat Rhino's ass for the world."

"My ass appreciates your confidence," Rhino retorted.

"Oh, it will," Zeph winked.

Odin interrupted, "You hear what Trip did the other day?"

"No," Zeph grunted as he flopped on a bench and nodded at Bo. "What'd his dumb ass get up to this time?" Trip was infamous for making stupid decisions before a fight. He'd gotten dumped by two trainers already for it.

"Went to Reno on a bender—"

"Jesus," Rhino snorted.

"—picked up a couple cheap hookers—" Odin continued.

"Sex workers," Zeph reminded him.

"Whatever. Picked up something—not cash—to pay them in..."

Zephyr stared. "What the fuck?"

"Only he's a dumbass, so he picked a cop and got busted. He's in a holding cell right now. Freddy ain't bailing him out. His girlfriend is *pissed*."

"Freddy?"

"Oh, yeah. His new trainer."

"About to be old trainer, again," Zeph rolled his eyes. "Jesus. We're a big deal, but we ain't rock stars."

"Speak for yourself." Rhino jumped on the spot and warmed up, stretching and bending.

Zeph grinned, then started his own stretches. The atmosphere down here was nice—not aggressive and hostile like people thought it would be between the fighters. Up at the top levels, they had separate locker rooms, but they also had one or two fights in a night. This was the midlist of fights, but heavily promoted. A win here meant good things for your career.

"You ready?"

"Always." Then, Rhino hesitated and tossed him a frown. "Not feeling so good today, though."

"The better to kick your ass, dude." Zeph eyed him, gauging if he meant a little nauseous or actually about to pass out.

He seemed okay, and he responded to the banter as always. "Always about my ass. Find a new obsession."

"But my shrine is almost complete." Zeph dropped to the floor for a few one-handed pushups.

Rhino had never admitted to nerves before, but this was a bigger night than most. The guy had a lot of career pressure on him, just like Zeph did.

They separated naturally minutes before the fight, each of their trainers giving them the last-minute pep talk and guidance, reminding them what openings to look for. Zeph passed along what Rhino had said, but Bo reminded him it could well be a feint—an attempt to make him look weak before he rebounded in the second round.

He'd stick to the game plan, then.

The roar of the crowd as they ascended the stairs would never grow old. The adrenaline from every little pre-fight moment—entering the cage, greeting the referee, playing up to the crowd...

Zeph was fucking high off it, but not so high he couldn't remember the one little, yet huge, difference tonight: River. He tried to look around for River in the crowd. He had a vague idea where he'd be sitting, since he'd scored him the tickets, but it was hard to see and he only had a few seconds to do it.

He spotted him only from the shock of platinum-blond hair and managed the briefest grin before he was out of time.

Zeph's world narrowed to Rhino, and vice versa. Even the referee, right there in their peripheral vision, couldn't punch through the surging adrenaline, the raw testosterone-fueled fighting instinct that made his head spin and his buddy look like the Goliath to be wrestled.

They circled each other once, twice, and then Rhino went for a quick hit to the torso, testing his limits.

Zeph dodged and landed an uppercut in response, testing right back to judge his speed today. The blow barely glanced off Rhino's shoulder, but it must have hit him right as he was shifting balance, because Rhino went down hard.

The audience would hate Zeph to take him down so fast in the first round, and it wasn't a clean fight if he pressed now, but he followed. He hit his knees by Rhino to make sure he wasn't trying to sweep his legs out from under him.

But Rhino wasn't even looking at him. His eyes were squeezed shut, his expression a grimace at first.

Time slowed as Rhino's expression softened and the fight went out of his body.

The fight half-forgotten, Zeph grabbed the front of Rhino's shirt. The audience roared in disapproval, expecting a dirty hit now, expecting the round to end this soon. Zeph ignored them and shook Rhino once.

He didn't respond.

Shit.

Before Zeph could even raise his hand to alert the referee, the man was there, pressing between them, and then there were medical staff.

Rhino wasn't getting back up. The fight was over. The ring doctor was beside him, working busily on his pulse, his breathing, talking to him and leaning in close. The stretcher was there, and a couple more nurses? Attendants? Some people were there.

Zeph was forgotten, only a couple of feet back but utterly out of the picture.

While he worked, the referee turned game show host, apologizing to the audience for whatever they'd missed in the pre-fight medical clearance. He started telling an anecdote from the locker room earlier.

He was distracting them from the truth that was sinking into Zeph's brain, slowly but with the catatonic torpor of an ice cube on his palm. By the time it melted, Zeph was numb but utterly certain. Staring at his friend's face, he knew it before the ambulance attendants even arrived.

Rhino was dead.

Zeph crouched on the ring floor as Rhino was finally hustled out of the ring for a futile ambulance trip. His eyes fixated on one little detail—the limp, taped-up hand that slipped free from the gurney before Rhino was strapped in.

Then he was covered with a blanket and there were staff members urging him to his feet and out of the ring while they reset, prepared for the next fight. Glossed over what had just happened, until the news broke later.

Dead. He'd been talking to him minutes ago, threatening him, shooting the shit like they did before every fight.

And now he was gone.

Zeph's brain couldn't reconcile it. In seconds, one of the toughest men he knew was gone.

By the time he tipped his head back to drink the sugary crap they were giving him, it was much too late to keep the shock from setting in.

Zeph swallowed the rest of the drink and rolled his head back, ignoring their questions as he gripped the side of the familiar post-fight medical table. Of course he knew his damn name and age. He hadn't gotten a concussion, he'd killed a man.

Somehow, he'd killed Rhino.

Thirty-Five

RIVER

"Can he go yet?"

River was a thorn in Bo's side and he knew it, but he didn't want Zeph sticking around here a minute longer than he had to. He'd found his way to the stairs by the locker room before security stopped him, and he'd had to wait until Bo happened to pass by before he could flag him down.

Bo had taken him down to the fluorescent-lit hallway under the place where the locker rooms were, and where River wasn't sure he'd ever been more out of place. Luckily he'd chosen skinny jeans, Converse, and a clingy t-shirt today, not wanting to deal with a worked-up crowd if someone decided to play amateur hour fag-bashing in the parking lot.

"After he gets out of this medical, yes." Bo was leaning against the wall on the other side of the door, his arms tightly folded.

River nodded slowly. He wanted to ask how long that would be, but he didn't want to push. He had no idea how well Bo had known the other guy, or if he was upset purely for Zeph's sake, or what the repercussions of this would be on their careers.

This couldn't be a common occurrence, because nobody down here seemed to know what to do. The other fighters must have found out, because when they passed River to head up to the cage, both of them and their trainers looked… well, not jazzed like everyone else had when they emerged onto the surface to step into the octagonal cage.

He was flying in the dark, his sole focus Zeph.

"I guess there's no drug tests or whatever…"

"They might do them anyway," Bo muttered. He looked like he was half in another universe, staring past River. "Procedure."

River winced and nodded. "Yeah." He hoped not, because he had no idea how long *that* took.

Just as he was losing the battle to resist asking how long Bo thought it would be, the door rattled.

It was Zeph, his eyes landing first on Bo, then River. His shoulders slumped with—relief? River hoped that was it. "I'm clear to leave."

Bo eyed Zeph, then squeezed his shoulders and patted his cheek in the manly, encouraging kind of way River had never quite mastered. "Take a couple cheat days. Call me when you're ready to come back to the gym. I'll kick your ass if you sneak in tomorrow."

"Yes, sir," Zeph chuckled, but the noise was hollow. He leaned in for a back-clapping half-hug.

Bo followed up, "River, you taking him home?" When River nodded, he offered him a small smile and nod. "Good. Thanks."

"Thanks," Zeph echoed to River, his gaze finally turning

to him. God, he was a mess. It wasn't hard to tell, especially if you knew him even a little.

River didn't address anything yet, though. Had to get him home first, at least, and probably wait until tomorrow. Zeph being Zeph, he'd need at least a day to get his head around this. "Of course. C'mon, let's take a ride in *my* car for a change."

With Zeph doing the Vegas trip driving, he hadn't gotten to show off his sexy little red Mazda to his new lover before. Hopefully it would keep his mind off all this shit for a few minutes, at least.

It did, at least, give Zeph a minute as he admired it and questioned River on the specs. *Typical boy.* River resisted the urge to smile as he made Zephyr Google the answers to his questions.

Then, he went quieter again.

Of course Zeph felt bad about himself—if he blamed himself for unrelated deaths, having even a small hand in Rhino's death had to be wrecking him from the inside out. And he looked lost, because he probably didn't even have the emotional tools to figure out how he felt about it.

River took Zeph's hand and played with his fingers while he drove, asking him whether he had normal groceries in the house. It took Zeph a few moments to realize he was teasing him about his training diet, but when he did manage to answer, it sounded like he did.

Good. That was one less thing to worry about.

When they pulled up to Zeph's apartment, River took a visitor parking spot so he could walk Zeph to the door and get him settled into his apartment.

This time, it was Zeph who reached for his hand first.

They walked, hand-in-hand, to the elevator, then up to the apartment door.

When Zeph was inside, River kept his shoes on as Zeph started to take his jacket off, then realized he didn't have one on and just patted his front.

"If you'd rather be alone today, I'll leave, but otherwise I want to stay," River told Zeph.

Zeph reached for his hand again and shook his head. "Stay. If you want."

"Of course." River kicked off his shoes and pulled Zeph against him by looping his arms around his waist. He leaned into him and scratched his back as they swayed together.

Zeph managed a smile at him, then pulled him toward his bedroom. "Want a glass of water or anything?"

"Nah." River eyed him. "You could probably use one, though."

"I'll be fine." Zeph's voice still sounded strange, like it wasn't quite coming from that big spirit of his.

God. River wanted to broach the subject, but it was still way too close. What he needed right now was escape. So he kept his lips zipped as they headed for Zeph's room and stripped off for bed.

"You're incredibly sexy in, uh…" Zeph gestured toward him vaguely, his brows pinching.

River's lips quirked. "In nothing?"

"That too. I meant, uh, whatever you'd call normal… I mean, typical… boy clothes?" Zeph's voice rose slightly as he eyed River cautiously.

River snorted with amusement. He'd heard a lot worse, and from people he didn't love.

Love.

He didn't dwell on the word. He loved a lot of people, after all.

"Sure, you can call them that," River agreed. "I know. Wearing girly things isn't to be sexier, even though I'm hot as fuck in them," he winked.

Zeph nodded and murmured, "Yeah, you are."

River winked. "It's because it feels more *me* that day."

"So is it, uh, a trans thing?" Zeph flopped onto the bed and offered an arm.

Oh. He wants to do this conversation now? I suppose it's a good way of distracting him...

River followed Zeph to the bed and flopped down onto the outstretched arm, letting Zeph pull him in against him. "Not strictly. I mean, technically I am. I'm not cis. If people ask, I say I'm nonbinary. But I'm also a guy. I'm okay with my body, if that's what you're worried about," he teased Zeph, drawing his fingers along his ribs one at a time.

"It was a concern," Zeph admitted with a low chuckle.

"*Man* doesn't... strictly fit me, but it fits better than *woman* does, even though I like drag, and I like wearing dresses and makeup, and I like kayaking and sexy fast cars, and... bad Chinese food," River shrugged helplessly, trying to get his sentence under control. "I mean, it doesn't have anything to do with what I wear, or what I like to do."

"Yeah." Zeph propped his cheek on his fist, his elbow on the pillow as he listened.

River furrowed his brow, trying to figure out how to condense what he wanted to say. "I'm neither, but I'm okay with people assuming I'm a man, or a drag queen, or whatever the fuck they wanna say."

"When did you know? That you were trans, or... nonbinary... or whatever you want to call it? That you're you?"

River cupped Zeph's cheek and rubbed his thumb along his jaw to show his appreciation for Zeph trying to echo his words. "God, for sure? Since I was a teen, I guess. As a kid, I played with pretty much every toy, I wanted to wear anything, I... pushed boundaries, I guess. I didn't give a fuck if nobody else was like me."

"Much like now," Zeph teased, his dark eyes fond.

River couldn't look away from that sweet and—dare he think it?—*adoring* gaze. "Yeah," he murmured. "And as a teen, it got worse. It got harder, because I didn't know if I *did* like my body, or anything. But I eventually kinda realized it wasn't that I didn't like my body, or being a man, it was just that that was the option everyone else wanted for me."

"So you were trying to resist what everyone else told you to do," Zeph surmised with a quiet nod. "Doesn't sound at all like you."

River snorted with laughter and smacked Zeph's chest. "Shut up."

"You shut up," Zeph retorted, rolling over on top of him and tickling his sides.

Caught by surprise, River yelped, then squealed and slapped at Zeph's hands. "Nonono, it's too—Jesus!" He dissolved in laughter, too weak to even wrestle Zeph off him. "Y-you asshole!"

"I can be," Zeph agreed, laughing richly as his fingers found the sensitive spots along his ribs and sides. He didn't give River a moment to breathe.

"Ohhhh my god," River giggled, gasping for breath as tears pricked his eyes and he squirmed, arching off the bed. "I hate you."

"Bet you don't."

"Fucker. Argh!" Zeph had pinched both nipples at once,

sending a quick wave of pain crashing through River. It was immediately followed by the intense heat of realizing Zeph's body was pressed up against his.

More importantly, Zeph's cock was nestled against his, half-hard and swelling. But at least he wasn't tickling him anymore. He let go and brushed his hands down River's chest, flicking the nipples again with his index fingers.

River gasped, trying to catch his breath as heat thrilled through his nerves. "Kinky bastard. You like seeing me all helpless?"

"And squirming under me," Zeph murmured, winking. Then he frowned slightly, his touch more... reverent. He looked like he never wanted to let go of River, just in case.

No wonder. River nudged Zeph, then grabbed his shoulders to push him over onto his side.

He rolled their bodies over until he was on top, running his hands from Zeph's hips up to his shoulders.

River knew what made Zeph tick. He knew what a big heart he kept hidden under that gruff exterior, and how playful he was, too. He knew Zeph's not-so-strange hot buttons—religion and family. He knew how fucking fiercely loyal he was, and how blindly he'd protect anyone he felt he could help.

It was time for Zeph to let River take care of him for the moment. If comfort was what Zeph needed, River could give him that.

"God, you're sexy," River whispered to break both their trains of thought. "I'm going to suck on that big, hot cock of yours and then ride it like there's no tomorrow."

Zeph's mouth opened, and River bit back a smile of satisfaction. That was something else he knew about him: how easy it was to turn him on with a few well-chosen dirty words. "Fuck, yes. Do it."

River grinned. "Is our no-condom agreement still…?"

"Yeah. Yeah, I didn't… with anyone else. You?"

River shook his head. The asshole hadn't had the courtesy to get out of his head after turning him down, so, no. There hadn't been anyone else. He doubted there would be for a while. The sex with Zeph was too fucking good to replace.

Zeph raised his brows, then smirked. "Huh. I see."

"Shut up," River grumbled. He was *not* actually admitting that to Zeph. He scooted down the bed instead, grinding their dicks together for a moment before he kissed along his chest and stomach.

He didn't waste time wrapping his lips around the head of his favorite cock, swiping his tongue along and around it.

"Fuck," Zeph hissed, wrapping his hand around the back of River's head but not pushing. He was too polite for that… until River teased it out of him.

River swallowed the throbbing shaft, pushing all the way to the back of his throat. God, he was glad his gag reflex was long since gone. He loved having a man's cock filling his mouth and throat, and Zeph tasted goddamn divine. He could happily suck his dick all day.

Especially when Zeph made those sounds of need, his breathing hitching and hips pushing up into Zeph now and then. Like he needed to move, but couldn't bring himself to do it.

I've got you.

River wrapped his hand around the base of his shaft and pulled his hand up with his lips, squeezing tightly as he bobbed his head.

Zeph's eyes were closed, his mouth open. "River," he gasped. "Fuck, you're good."

River desperately wanted to kiss those sexy lips. He moaned in response, lapping at the head before pulling his head back. He stroked Zeph a few times, then leaned over to grab lube. "Don't want you coming before I even get on you."

"N-No," Zeph agreed with a breathy laugh, his hands rising to River's body. Every time he looked at him, it was like he couldn't help but touch.

River slid two fingers inside himself, even if he was pretty sure spit and determination could do the job. He grinned as Zeph's hands wandered down to his thighs, then up to his chest and shoulders again. The whole time, Zeph couldn't stop watching his fingers between his thighs.

"You like to watch," River teased.

Zeph's cheeks flushed and he snorted, but he didn't defend himself. "Not my fault you're the hottest thing… ever."

"No colorful analogy?"

"Since, I don't know, sliced bread? Give me a break. My brain's short-circuiting," Zeph groaned. He was holding his cock now, sliding it between River's cheeks, bumping it against his hand.

River suppressed a gasp at how much he wanted it. Once his fingers were loose, he grabbed a tissue and wiped the lube off them, humming under his breath. "Do I let you sit up and kiss me, or not?"

Zeph was already pressing into him, stretching him open and sliding inside in a single motion. The upward jerk of his hips made River gasp and sit down hard on him.

"*Fuck!*" River breathed out, his head spinning.

"Shh. S'okay," Zeph breathed, his hand rising to cup River's cheek. "You good?"

River turned his head to kiss Zeph's palm and nodded as the sparks of pain and disorientation faded, the heat building deep in his stomach again.

There it was: his prostate being rubbed with every gentle thrust, his cock throbbing in response. The nerves along his body lit up as Zeph started pushing up into him. Fuck, his nipples were sensitive, and even his cheek… every brush of Zeph's palm against his skin made him twitch with pleasure.

"I'm supposed to be doing the work," he complained after a moment.

Zeph chuckled. "By all means."

River shifted so he could brace himself better on his knees, then cupped Zeph's cheeks in both of his and leaned down far enough to kiss him hard, just once.

"Mmmph." Zeph pushed himself up to prop himself against the headboard, pulling River's hips along with him to keep their bodies locked together.

On second thought, River wouldn't complain about his every gasp and moan being swallowed by those beautiful lips.

And did Zeph ever ravish his lips with sucking, sweet kisses at first, then harder, needier, open-mouthed, *hungry* kisses…

He pushed himself up and down hard, leaning back to catch his breath and bracing himself on Zeph's knee as his head rolled back.

Zeph leaned in to lick his throat instead and he whimpered, his whole body tightening for a moment.

"Fuck, you're turned on," Zeph whispered, his hand lightly curling around River's shaft. It was so fucking sensitive he squirmed at first, but within a few strokes, River was back in his rhythm.

His pleasure was in Zeph's hands as he squeezed tight around him, pushing as hard and fast as he could.

And he couldn't stop smiling. He *loved* sex with Zeph. It was fucking *fun*, even when it was hot and fast with no time for shared chuckles over their memories or their clumsiness or weird-ass ideas like whipped cream.

Zeph moved with him, half-dazed and staring up at him like he was the center of his world.

Oh, yeah. That was the other thing he loved about sex with Zeph: the way Zeph never seemed to be thinking of anyone, or even any*thing* else but him.

Zeph tightened his grip around River's dick and he caught his breath as his body tensed. His nails dug into Zeph's shoulders as he lost his rhythm for a second, then redoubled his efforts.

Fuck, he needed every inch of that hot dick in him when he came, needed Zeph's taste on his lips…

"Yes!" River whimpered, rolling his head back. Fuck, he was so close he didn't even have time to think twice. He just slammed his hips down a few more times, then clenched tight around Zeph as he came, painting both their stomachs in a sticky, passionate mess. "Yeah, fucking *yes*, Zeph… fuck, you fill me up," he moaned, slumping against Zeph.

Zeph's arm was right there around his waist, holding him against his body. But the way Zeph's hips stuttered, pushing up into him, he could tell he was so fucking close.

"Come, too, baby," River whispered against his neck as Zeph wrung every last drop from him.

Zeph grabbed his hips and pushed up into him a few

more times, his breathing quickly becoming low growls of need.

"Fill me up. Show me I'm yours," River whispered, pressing kisses against the salty sweetness of his neck. "I can feel you getting there. Fucking show me how much you need me."

"I… *yes!*" Zeph growled, crushing their bodies together as his hips slammed up into River, erratic but deep.

Wet and sticky inside and out, River gave a satisfied grin, pushing away from Zeph enough to watch the pleasure bleed into contentment on his face. "Oh, God, yeah," River whispered. "That's hot."

Zeph wrapped his arms around his waist as he softened and slid free. "You're a fucking sex god. Or demon. Something."

"I'm a greedy little fucker for your cock," River agreed easily, winking when Zeph gave him a startled look. "What?"

Zeph breathed out a quick laugh. "I don't think I'll ever get used to the things you say."

"Good," River winked, pulling himself off Zeph and grabbing tissues. When they were clean enough to roll under the covers together, they did.

Zeph was out like a light within minutes. River lay awake for a few more minutes to listen to his even, steady breathing before he let himself drift off, too.

I hope he'll be okay.

Was that an arm or a leg around his waist? After a moment, Zeph decided it was definitely an arm, because he felt two icy feet buried between his own to leach his heat like a damn parasite.

He couldn't be angry, though. All Zeph felt was wonder at how lucky he was to have River wrapped around him while he awoke. The peaceful moment of listening to River's steady breathing, watching sunlight filter in through the morning blinds, taking note of every spot where their bodies brushed —nearly from head to toe...

This could be his reality every day.

And then it wasn't.

His world came crashing down as soon as his mind awoke enough to offer a reminder of yesterday.

Yesterday: the day everything had changed, once again.

The look on Rhino's face right before he died. The fear, confusion, pain. Like he'd needed help but hadn't known how to ask.

It was like a kick to the fucking stomach. No, worse—

Zeph had had plenty of those that didn't make emotion swell inside him until his skin fucking strained. He wanted to peel his own existence away, layer by layer.

They'd told him last night it wasn't his fault—the glancing blow had no more caused it than the moon phase. He'd already been in the middle of medical distress.

But Rhino was dead now, and he hadn't been before, and the difference was that he'd gotten up that day to fight *him*.

Zeph wasn't any more superstitious than he was religious. He knew it was all a bunch of damn coincidences. But when he thought about it, it was another fucking tally on the list of people who'd died from exposure to him.

That was what hurt the most: he couldn't be trusted to keep his own buddy safe in the ring. Maybe he could have stopped the fight earlier. He could have told someone that Rhino hadn't been feeling well, and Rhino could have gone to the hospital instead of dying in the cage.

It hurt so badly Zeph couldn't breathe, even with River's breath against his neck and the warmth of the sunlight that streamed across his sheets, soaking through them to settle into his bones.

None of it made a damn difference.

He couldn't keep anyone safe near him, least of all River. How long would it be before something happened that he couldn't stop? How long before he hurt River, or worse? Before he lost his life to some fucking out-of-control asshole like him?

For all Zeph tried to keep his life organized and tidy and clean, his past was still there. However hard he fought, he couldn't keep the ghosts of his past from breathing down his neck. Jesus, even in Vegas, *George* had shown up for the first time since he'd left that foster home.

It terrified him, the idea that he could bring harm to River just by being around him. Hell, maybe that asshole stalker had first come over because of him, not River. Maybe he'd been the competition the guy had wanted to overpower. It made as much sense as anything else.

Zeph was a liability. Everything could be his fault, and nothing was safe.

He shifted and rolled away from River, pushing the sheets off. When River yawned, stretched, and tried to pull him in again, he pushed River's hand away.

River pushed himself to sit up. "Morning."

"Yeah." Zeph kept his eyes on the dresser as he stretched, not looking back at River.

"You all right?"

Zeph grunted.

River sighed, and then the sheets rustled and the bed shifted. River tried to lean against him, putting his chin on his shoulder.

"You can't stop touching me," Zeph grunted and pushed himself to his feet to pace over to the dresser.

River didn't say anything, just watched him. The silence was more disconcerting than an answer.

"Cat got your tongue?" Zeph finally asked, his voice tight even to his own ears.

River answered, his voice even, "Is there anything to say?"

"Nope." Zeph pulled open drawers, fishing out his under-wear, a t-shirt, and jeans. "You should get home before we make even more mistakes."

"More?"

"Like getting attached." Zeph shot River a look over his shoulder. "I was right before, you know."

River wasn't giving him an inch. He kept asking questions. "About?" was the latest one.

Zeph's jaw gritted in annoyance. "About us. It didn't work out for a reason before."

"Because you moved."

"If we'd cared that much, we would have stayed in touch," Zeph pointed out, sitting on the edge of the bed to pull his clothes on one piece at a time.

River didn't touch him again, but he sat close by. "That was a long time ago."

"We haven't changed that much." Goddammit, however much Zeph tried, he couldn't seem to. "You're still fucking everything that looks at you without getting weirded out. I'm still fighting everything that moves."

"You're fighting me," River told him, his voice low. "And I'm only fucking you."

Zeph paused as he pulled on his t-shirt, then finished pulling it over his torso and turned to River. "Yeah, maybe." It wasn't like he could help it. Fighting was all he knew how to do. "You should find someone else."

"Someone better than you?"

Zeph flinched but nodded. That was a good way of putting it, even if it pissed him off to hear it.

"I was expecting this," River told him, which wasn't what he'd expected.

"What?"

"You pushing me away." River sighed and pushed his hair to the side, playing with it for a moment as he gazed across the room, then finally looked at him again. "Okay. Here's the thing."

Zeph instinctively folded his arms. It didn't sound good, whatever was coming.

"I was giving you a free pass before because fuck knows you've been through stuff. Everyone needs time to learn how to deal with that. But you're pushing me away again. If I leave, this time, I'm not reaching out again."

Exactly what Zeph had figured. Everyone said they'd be there for him when he needed it, or they'd stick with him, but who was willing to do that when the *real* him came out? Nobody. Not even River.

"I *want* to make it work with you," River murmured, pulling on his own clothes in quick, efficient movements. Those slender hands danced up his buttons, buttoning up the clingy black over-shirt. "But I'm not going to do a back-and-forth fucked-up TV drama. It might not be obvious, and I don't act like it to someone who isn't looking close enough, but I have a bit too much self-respect for that."

"Right. So, you're leaving." Zeph brushed aside all the rest of the pretty, meaningless words.

River eyed him, then scratched his nose and pushed himself to his feet. "If you wanna hear it that way."

"Not many other ways to take that," Zeph retorted, pulling open the bedroom door and heading for the kitchen.

He needed a drink of water to clear his head. Normally by this time he'd have had several, plus a protein shake and a good workout.

Now he was going out of his damn mind, trying not to think about what was going through River's head. Trying not to think about what was going through his *own* head.

When he leaned in the hallway again, River was pulling on his shoes. He wouldn't—couldn't—get closer.

"Right. See you, then," Zeph said, because it felt like someone needed to say *something*.

"I hope so." River straightened up and looked at him, that wide-open face inscrutable for once.

Goddammit, what was he *feeling*? What did he want from him?

Zeph wanted to throw something heavy, or lift something, or run ten miles. Anything to burn off the shit that was clouding his thinking. Something to cut through it and show him what he was supposed to do.

Instead, he just raised a hand slightly. And River just nodded, and left. And then, when he was alone, he slid slowly down the wall to sit on the floor of the hallway.

Now and then, I wish there were *a God out there I could pray to. Someone to tell me what the fuck I'm supposed to do.*

There were no signs, no voices breaking through the clouds and booming through his windows, *chase the man!* or *let him go!*

Instead, the clock ticked and ticked and ticked, and Zeph? Zeph was alone again.

Thirty-Seven

RIVER

River's world was crashing down.

For all he'd blustered back there at Zeph's place, he wasn't nearly as confident inside as he'd projected to Zeph. River wasn't sure whether he needed someone to slap him upside the head or hug him.

He wasn't even sure he could stick to the choice he'd told Zeph he was making.

River had parked outside Kyle and Nic's house, and seeing both cars home wasn't much reassurance. Maybe they were out at the park or something. But no, the blinds rustled and then the door opened.

River sighed, touched his face to make sure he had his shit together, and went to brush back his hair. When he realized he wasn't wearing his wig, he touched his ear instead, then headed up the sidewalk to the front door.

Nic was there, offering him a smile. "Hey. Come in. We've got pancakes." He was in just jeans and a t-shirt, barefoot. Oh, of course—it was Sunday morning.

"Fuck. I'm not disturbing you?"

"Nah. It's not our weekend with Kevin, and Kyle's doing *terrible* renditions of old theme songs. Thank God you came." Nic grinned.

Despite himself, River managed a smile. When he reached the front door, Kyle was there to sweep him into a hug while Nic ducked back into the kitchen to cook.

"Hey, darling. Juice or water?"

"Juice," River requested, letting Kyle pull him over to the couch. "Sorry I just showed up."

Kyle shrugged him off. "Boy trouble?"

Nic came back, bearing a glass of juice, and sat on his other side.

It felt a bit like a pair of avenging angels were about to go beat up Zeph, so he felt obligated to tell them, "It's not his fault."

"Uh huh," Kyle drawled. "Spill."

River started from the beginning: the self-defense lesson. How he'd been fine holding on and waiting until the fight was over. The fight, how it had gone well until it hadn't, and how shocked Zeph had been. Bringing Zeph home, and the fact they'd had totally comfort sex. And then... the abrupt shift to grumpy asshole Zeph that morning.

"He just told you to leave, basically?" Kyle's arms were folded. "What the fuck?"

"No, wait," Nic shushed his boyfriend. "You said you were leaving, and he said okay, pretty much?"

"More that," River admitted. He sighed and closed his eyes. "I don't know," he admitted to his palms as he rubbed his face. "I just... wanna know I'm doing the right thing."

"Well, he's still being a dick, so..." Kyle grumbled. He

looked so offended he was craning his neck back, like Zeph was standing in front of him offering him a handshake.

River admitted that with a shrug. "Yeah. He was trying to hit every button he could find."

"And that *is* a dick move," Nic interjected firmly, drawing both of their gazes. "But it doesn't mean you're giving up on him, does it?"

Kyle scoffed. "Of course he is! Aren't you?"

A few seconds of silence and their gazes on him and River had to look down. No, Nic was right—he wasn't. He didn't want to. Hell, if Zeph didn't come to him within a few months… weeks… maybe days…

"Shit. Jesus, you're stuck on him," Kyle sighed.

River nodded slightly, his throat tight.

"Why? I think you know."

Both Kyle and River stared at Nic, and then Kyle turned his gaze to River, too.

River's cheeks flushed as he looked down. "Yeah. I love him."

Kyle hissed under his breath, and then squeezed his knee. "Baby. I didn't know."

River shook his head slightly. "It…" He could say he didn't, either, but that wouldn't be true.

A part of him had, all those years ago, and maybe that part had never really stopped. But this time, he couldn't just walk away from it. If they'd used his move as an excuse to separate before, it might have been from starting to get too close to the emotional reality for them both: that there was something between them that was worth fighting for.

That they wanted to bare their hearts and souls to each other, and it utterly terrified them both for what River had thought were different reasons. But maybe they were one and the same: they were both scared of being hurt again.

"He's not… emotionally… uh," Nic waved a hand. "Adept."

"You can say that again," Kyle muttered. River cracked a smile at his long-time friend's interjection, but Nic ignored it.

"He's obviously not supposed to lash out at you, though."

"Agreed." Kyle nodded, squeezing River's shoulder now. "That's below the belt."

"Yeah. That's not cool, and you can totally put your foot down on that," Nic told him. "In fact, I think you have to for him to see that's not okay behavior. But I'm guessing he didn't have a stable living situation, or nice parents, or something before."

River hesitated. He didn't want to overshare, but yeah, that was an understatement from the little he knew: that Zeph had had several foster homes. He'd never said more than that.

"So he's learned this shit, and he needs to unlearn it. It's not your obligation to teach him. You can walk away now. And if he doesn't want to learn, I'd say you *should*," Nic added, eyeing Kyle, no doubt to quell his objections.

"Hmph." Kyle nodded.

River nodded slowly. "But… I love him. I don't want to just walk away again. I do that too much."

Kyle murmured, "Is this about him specifically, or you being lonely?"

Ouch. River shot him a quick look, then frowned. "Both, but… mostly him. I've been alone for plenty long enough without making the same mistake on the same guy over and over."

"Right," Nic nodded. "So if you stick by him, you need to make your rules clear and make them make sense to him: he can't piss you off when he's scared and he needs time to think about his feelings. Give him an out. Tell him how to get you to go away, and show him you'll stick by him if he doesn't take that out, and that you'll leave when he tells you to."

That actually sounded really simple, when he put it like that. River stared at Nic. "Right."

"He's not going to be easy to love," Nic added slowly, glancing at Kyle. "Those of us who've been… you know…"

"Fucked up," River supplied.

Kyle cracked up. "Yeah, we all have been. None of us are."

River glanced away for a moment. Fuck, his own outer shell of sassy snark and quips was the hardest to break, and Zeph had slipped inside with barely a sideways glance. There were a thousand easier guys to date if Zeph cared about social appearances, or what would happen to his career when people knew he was seeing a guy like *him*, who couldn't even play discreet for a day…

But something made Zeph come back to him. Maybe Zeph didn't understand it, much like River wasn't sure of all that kept him hooked on Zeph, coming back for another hit over and over.

"I love him," River whispered under his breath, and then he slowly shook his head. "Fuck."

Kyle slid his arm around his shoulders and Nic joined in from the other side.

"It's scary, isn't it?" Kyle asked quietly.

River blinked away the tears. For the first time in a long time, a man had him feeling vulnerable, and yeah, it was. Zeph was using that to try to get his space, but Nic was right.

It was an unhealthy coping mechanism, and he wasn't going to stand for it.

But in his rare moments where he was unguarded, and he wasn't second-guessing himself or trying to keep everything so tightly wound up it was a wonder he didn't snap, Zeph was everything River knew he could be.

Will he ever see that?

CHAPTER
Thirty-Eight

ZEPH

THREE, FOUR, FIVE... SHIT, HE WAS PUSHING TOO HARD. OH, well. It may as well be upper *and* lower body day. And core, while he was at it.

Zeph knew damn well his coping mechanisms weren't the best. Self-care was a hot bath after a good training session, not something he sat around and did with candles and yoga.

He *did* do yoga, but only under Bo's instruction to help him stay limber. He wouldn't dream of doing it to center his spirit or whatever the fuck most people did.

All he knew was exercise. As a kid, running miles at any new school with a track, and as a teen, working out in the backyard of whatever homes had one, and as a young adult, in the gym.

So working out, pushing his body to near-total collapse, was all he knew. He defaulted there when he didn't know what else to do, so it was what he was doing when Tristan called the first time. And the second time. And the third time.

At last, there was a knock on his door.

Zeph tried to ignore it as he wiped the sweat out of his eyes and dropped to his back on the mat.

Another, harder rap on the door sounded. It followed a pattern he recognized. *Aww, crap.*

"Hey, Zeph. I know you're lifting weights or something dumb." Tristan. "Open the damn door, don't make me use my spare key."

"I'm busy."

Tristan didn't relent. "Doing what?"

"Fucking a pretty blond thing," Zeph groused, flipping off the door.

"Right. Shave your palms, then, loser."

Ouch. Zeph couldn't help a quick snort, though. Nothing like a friend to lift your mood. He pushed himself slowly to his feet and made it to the door to pull it open.

"What?"

Tristan eyed him with a mix of annoyance and amusement, his lip lifting but eyes rolling. "Nice to see you, too."

"I'm busy," Zeph told him again.

Tristan jammed his toe in the door. "Don't even think of shutting that in my face."

"Well, now I'll be shutting it on your foot."

Tristan eyed him, then folded his arms. "You broke up."

"Well done, Sherlock."

"Officially?"

Technically, they hadn't said the words, but River's meaning had been clear enough. Zeph didn't answer, but his silence answered for him.

"Oh, so you're on some kind of *figure out how to feel things break*," Tristan supplied.

Zeph cast a glare down the hall and stepped back to let

Tristan in so his theatrical projection didn't send his personal business down to the end of the hall.

Tristan stepped inside and stayed in the entranceway, leaning there. "So?"

"I don't need your pity, *let's feel this out* talk," Zeph told him.

"What if I want to give it to you anyway?"

"Then you can fuck right off," Zeph pointed at the door, glaring at Tristan. He should know better by now than to fuck around with that kind of thing.

Tristan raised his eyebrow. "Look at you, Mr. Snarls. Feeling tougher now that you're not admitting to having feelings?"

Zeph folded his arms. "What do you want?"

"You to get over yourself, for a start," Tristan fired back. For a willowy little twig, he sure had an attitude.

"Oh, right. I couldn't possibly forget that with everyone reminding me I need to do it every five minutes," Zeph scoffed. Fuck 'em. They had no idea how much he had to get over.

"Man." Tristan caught Zeph's gaze and didn't look away or back down, even when Zeph glowered. "I know you've had a lot of bullshit other people have done to you. Your parents are gone, your friends died, you were in foster care, right? Abuse there, too? Don't give me that surprised look. Reading people is my job."

Zeph was more disconcerted than angry for a second, but it was a lot easier to fall back into resentment and glare now that Tristan had actually *said* those words out *loud*.

"They're not your fault. So why the fuck do you keep acting like they are?"

Zeph drew his brows together, about to say that he wasn't, and he wasn't even talking about them.

"You're punishing yourself for things other people did. To you, or to themselves. Why? Is it because you can't punish them?"

Zeph's fists curled tightly, but he wouldn't strike.

As if proving that very point, Tristan took a step closer, then another, until he rested a hand on Zeph's.

"You're a fucking machine in the cage, but you're still not the kind of man who would hit me, even now with me in your face telling you you're being an idiot, are you?"

Zeph had no idea what to even say in response. He just blinked, dumbly. He couldn't see where Tristan's argument was going.

"That's what I thought. So they didn't fuck you up *that* badly. You still care. You still like people. You love him, like it or not."

Zeph swallowed hard as the penny dropped.

"So cut out the bullshit and act like the guy you are, in here." Tristan tapped his chest once, then pushed away for the door. "And improve that attitude after you apologize to him for whatever you did and call me back, huh?"

"Fuck you, too." Zeph half-smiled, unable to help himself, at the balls on Tristan. His friend just turned his back and walked away on him. Dozens of fighters he knew would never risk that, even on a good day.

But Tristan knew him.

Tristan blew him a kiss and pulled open the door. "Love you too, asshole."

Like a deflated balloon, Zeph leaned on the wall when the door shut. For the second time, he found himself sitting on the floor of the hall, his eyes closed.

But this time, there was an inkling of *something* itching at him… an idea that maybe this wasn't the end of everything he and River had been building.

That maybe there was a way through.

All thanks to Tristan. Sheesh. That asshole couldn't just let him stew in misery, could he?

Damn it. I guess that's what friends are for.

Thirty~Nine

ZEPH

THROUGHOUT THE NIGHT AND THE NEXT DAY, ZEPH COULDN'T shake Tristan's words.

He'd had a few people love him—fickly, maybe—and plenty of people tell him he was an asshole. But at the same time? Never.

And Zeph knew that eventually, he was going to have to face the demons from his past before he could move on. He'd been running away from them for damn long enough, but their hold was still too strong. He was running in place, trying everything and anything to get them off his back.

So to speak. A shiver ran down his spine.

"Fucking friends," he muttered as he took out some energy on his protein shaker. He kept a hand tightly over the lid so he didn't get overly enthusiastic and coat his kitchen walls with protein powder and spinach. It had happened before.

Confronting old demons was *hard*, though. He wasn't sure he wanted to. It was way more comfortable to be alone, where nobody could hurt him.

But somehow, that wall had fallen. Pushing River away had already hurt him, and no matter what happened now, it was going to keep hurting. Running away from him even more? That would hurt him most of all.

Therapy was a bit of a stretch for him yet. He'd never seen himself being able to walk into an office and... well, spill his heart to some stranger. No way.

But he could find his own closure. He could go see those places that were etched in his brain. The ones that he consciously or unconsciously ran from, that he'd placed all the trauma into and boxed up tightly in the back of his brain.

Zeph hadn't been to any of them in years, and maybe that was part of the problem. They were blown out of proportion, like a kid looking up at his school building and thinking it was huge, only to see it as an adult and realize it was just a regular old building.

It didn't take nearly as long to drive to the first spot on his mini-tour as he'd thought—just forty minutes and Zeph was on the outskirts of Riverside, in a tiny residential street that he had to drive up and down.

It wasn't until his third pass, when he was seriously in danger of having some old Neighborhood Watch lady spy through her curtains, when he spotted the house where he'd grown up with his parents.

He hadn't even recognized it at first.

He parked out front and gazed at the faded green panels on the front, the single tree that still stood between the house and the road, the scrubby desert bushes by the driveway.

Zeph's memories from that stage of his life were patchy, but they fit into this house. It was just strange to see that tree here in front of him that he'd climbed as a kid, and that corner of the house where he'd hosed down his bike after a mud puddle contest, and the front door his mom had carried him through, half-asleep after a road trip.

Before he could dwell and make more of it than the place it was, Zeph pulled away in search of his first foster home. That was easy—he remembered the addresses for every one. Some freaky ability for a kid who couldn't add three numbers well.

Then, the spot Anton had crashed his car—unmarked by even a plain white cross, as per his parents' wishes—and then a church.

The church. Where he'd been abused.

Tristan had picked the right word, and he'd wielded it the same way he'd thrown words at River to try to crack him.

The difference was that he'd been trying to protect River from himself by hurting him, but Tristan had been trying to hurt him to protect him from himself. To get him to see this.

Fuck. The place was dingy and small and his skin still crawled at the thought of walking inside, but it was there. A real place, where people still went and smiled and bonded over stupid church luncheons.

Where *that* asshole might still work. For all the homework he did on every dodge and weave his opponents were known for, Zeph had never once been able to bring himself to Google Father Peters and make sure he wasn't a clergy member.

All that fight, and Tristan was right—he was aiming it at the wrong people.

If he didn't get control of himself now, it meant that the bad people won. Not just the people who'd unintentionally hurt him—Anton, crashing his car in a moment of fear—but the people who'd hurt him on purpose.

Who had known exactly how bad they had to be fucking up a child.

Father Peters, George. People like *them* won.

Zeph was a fighter. He'd made it his damn career, and now he was starting to realize why. But it wasn't his life.

He wasn't going to fight everyone and everything. That was like when the enemy—the opponent—had you pinned to the mat and you wasted your energy swinging at places they could defend, letting them choke you out.

As he started his car, Zeph's brain was a mile away—or maybe a few decades back, he couldn't tell.

But he knew one thing for sure: he wanted to move on.

CHAPTER

Forty

RIVER

Slinking out to the dumpster with an overstuffed bag of trash was always embarrassing. River tried to wait until later in the evening, when people wouldn't judge him for the pizza boxes poking out of the garbage and the ice cream cartons in his recycling bags.

Like he was an uncouth bachelor living off freezer food. Which he was, but only because he didn't have the time or energy to cook. Except he did, but… well, fuck it.

He was going through half a breakup without really knowing what was going on.

"It's complicated," so to speak. Facebook would have a ball with this, but he hadn't really been logging on lately. He hadn't been on the scene, so he wasn't sure what he was missing.

He *did* miss the warning signs until the door was all the way open, though.

River wasn't alone.

His stalker was there.

He'd found him again.

And the stocky man was rushing for the door, his face twisted into some grimace of... lust? Rage?

Oh, God. It hit River that he didn't know what this man wanted from him. Did he want to teach him a lesson for hitting on the wrong straight man? Was he attracted to him and full of self-loathing for it, lashing out at him? Was he just flat-out attracted, trying to win him over by force if not by charm?

What was he going to have to defend himself against?

He couldn't get the bag of trash out of the doorway in time to slam the apartment door shut, and his stalker took advantage of that to push them back into the apartment, kicking the bag out of the way to shut the door.

River reeled as he realized *this was really happening*. He was there, smelling like beer and cigarette smoke, crowding River's personal space.

His arm went around River's neck, pulling him back, away from the door. Back where he couldn't call for help and expect anyone to hear.

River didn't even know the man's name. He just knew that every card, every message he'd left had gotten worse and worse. He had no idea what the end game was, but he knew he didn't want to go down without a fight.

So he turned his chin into his collarbone, grabbed the man's elbow, and twisted his body away. But the man was bigger than him, and when he forced him to his knees, he grabbed River's waist to pull him down, too.

It was the school yard all over again. He had Brett's fist in his face while Jared tried to pull his skirt off.

But this time, he was older, stronger, better-trained. This time, there were no detentions to avoid.

And the stakes were so much higher: kill or be killed.
"Not this time, asshole."
River fought.

CHAPTER
Forty~One
ZEPH

Church Heights: the name of probably a thousand other graveyards in this state alone, but there was only one Zeph knew about.

This was his last stop: the place where his parents were buried. He hadn't been there in years, so even though he knew exactly where the place was relative to the city, it took a long time for him to find their graves in the fading light of the day.

The cemetery itself was well-kept: the grass was short, and there was no litter. The headstones were tidy, and there were no dead plants or tattered memorabilia at the other graves.

When Zeph finally found the right row, he knew it because his memory was vaguely activated by the shape of the headstones along the row. He walked down it toward his parents' graves and stopped at the two plain plots right next to one another.

They looked sad and empty. There were no flowers there, no stone or metal ornaments near the headstones.

Zeph shoved his hands in his pockets as he crouched in front of the graves, then sank down to kneel there.

He was alone today—nobody else wandering the rows to sightsee, or enjoy the views of the city from here. Not even to visit their own ancestors' graves.

Years since his last visit. Fuck, and probably nobody else from his family had bothered stopping by, either. It wasn't like they were close enough to have kept in touch with him, the only living one, or checked in on him… they sure as hell wouldn't bother coming here.

He closed his eyes and let his hands brush through the grass on each grave, his eyes welling up.

"I'm sorry," he managed before his breathing grew too uneven to speak. He ducked his head to hide his tears out of habit, even if he was alone.

Zeph had never had a breakdown like this, and all because of a couple of fucking plain graves.

But this was the last thing he had of them. He'd gotten nothing from their estate; if he had, he would have had to ditch it when he left the last foster home anyway, so it was probably a good thing.

For a long time, he'd been angry at them. It wasn't rational, but it was the only emotion he'd been able to understand, so he'd clung to it.

He'd hated them for leaving him.

But it had sunk in now, harder than ever: they hadn't exactly had a choice. He was positive they hadn't *wanted* to, and given any choice, they'd have done anything to stay with him.

It was completely unfair that they hadn't been able to. It hurt worse than anything else he could think of, but no wonder… he'd never let himself think about the injustice of it.

And when the pain cleared, when he could breathe again, and when he could think straight, it started to become obvious what he had to do.

This was the event that had started everything else spiraling out of control. If not for this, he would have had parents and not foster homes; if not for foster homes, he would never have met George or Father Peters. If not for that, he wouldn't have met Anton sneaking out from church, too. He wouldn't have driven himself into fighting, into watching Rhino as he died. He wouldn't have been afraid to let River love him.

But he still had a choice. Goddamn it, he *did*, and it might utterly scare him, but he could only pray River was still there, waiting halfway between them with open arms. If not, he'd chase him down, and show River that he was willing to *not* fight.

He was in control now.

Feeling lighter, he rose to his feet and shoved his hands into his pockets again, then nodded.

His parents would want him to be happy, and nothing worth doing ever came easy. He didn't lift weights until he felt rosy and fresh-faced, but until he wanted to throw up. He didn't eat foods that tasted good to cut before a weigh-in. However unfamiliar, he could learn this, too.

It was time to win back his man.

CHAPTER
Forty-Two

ZEPH

"I'm sorry for what I said." Zeph closed his car door and lowered his voice to a mutter, so nobody could overhear. "I shouldn't have... tried to... ugh. Fuck. Words." Maybe he'd just be spontaneous.

But the second he got to the top of the stairs, Zeph knew something was wrong. There was a trash bag outside River's apartment, and although the door was closed, he heard a sound.

Then another—a distinct *thud*. He knew the sounds of a fight anywhere. And he also knew River wasn't the type to fight just anyone, which meant...

He's back.

Zeph crossed the distance between the staircase and River's door in less time than it took to draw his breath.

"River!"

He tested the knob before he kicked down the door. Good thing, because it started to swing open, and River's damage deposit probably didn't cover a door.

The creep from the bar, all six-foot-something of his ugly ass, was pushing River up against the door to his bedroom, a hand going to River's throat, but the door opening distracted him and he looked back over his shoulder.

"Fuck off," he growled.

But Zeph ignored him. He didn't give a shit what *he* said. It was River's quiet, "Zeph," that sounded like a prayer and a plea in one.

God knew how long he'd been there. River looked exhausted, and so did the other guy, but River had held his own.

Goddamn, Zeph was proud of him.

He snarled as he crossed the hall in a few quick paces, blocking this guy's route to the door. He was not getting away again.

And more importantly, he was never laying a hand on River again.

Between them, they flipped him to the floor in a few seconds, and when he tried to get away, River stepped on his stomach to keep him there.

"You fucking *creep*," Zeph snarled as the asshole grabbed his legs and tried to pull him down.

Fine, he wanted to take this to the mat? He'd show him a floor game.

Zeph sank to his knees, parried the blows at him, and landed two in quick succession on either side of the fucker's face. He took a few hits to his shoulder and stomach, but he doled them out faster than he took them, leaving the other man's already-bloodied face even more raw.

River was going to be bruised, too. Fuck. Zeph *ached* at the thought, much worse than a hit could ever hurt him.

Zeph wanted to tear this guy in two, but he didn't deserve

that mercy. He deserved to be ground through the legal system until his face was plastered everywhere, and he was forced to repeat in court every creepy fucking word he'd sent to River on the sly.

"I've got him," River snarled. "You call the cops."

"Are you sure?"

In answer, River just gave him a small, dangerous smile.

Zeph actually felt a shiver run down his spine. For that second, River looked like a fighter. *Shit*, he had no idea how incredibly attractive that was. He managed a quick nod and got off him, resisting the urge to spit on the little twerp as he grabbed his phone to call the cops.

He stayed between the guy and the door, just in case he *did* try to run for it.

And, true to his word, River stood watch over him. His bruised knuckles were locked together in tight fists. He looked like he wanted to throttle the guy. The guy wasn't breathing a word now, but every time he moved, River stepped on one of his body parts, so no wonder.

Just one hit, and I can knock him out.

"911."

"We have a break-and-enter and assault by my boyfriend's stalker. We subdued him. He's here on the floor. Babe, what's your address?"

River offered him a half-smile, then gave his address.

It took Zeph a second to realize which words had slipped from his mouth and he winced in apology.

But River just shook his head slightly, then returned his gaze to the guy on the floor.

Well, one thing was for sure: Zeph had fucked up, but River had never looked at him with *that* expression.

It looked like River wanted to do just about everything

Zeph wanted to do to the stalker. This creepy fucker was going to be *glad* to be in custody as soon as the cops showed up.

Forty-Three

RIVER

THE COPS WERE FINALLY, *FINALLY* GONE.

And they'd taken the guy—Jack Pearson, a perfectly ordinary name for a guy who'd seemed larger-than-life in the fearful place River had been mentally stuck in for weeks now —with them.

If everything went as it should, Jack was never going to bother him again. The detective in charge of his stalking case had already been alerted. Jack had looked downright scared when the cops took him into custody. He had a hell of a long road ahead of him, and *good*.

River was tired. So fucking tired he couldn't even describe it. The exhaustion dragged at his very bones, slowing his movements and his thoughts.

But more than that, he felt... wrong.

Not just from the words Jack had whispered when they were fighting. Not just from the words that still flashed in his head from every card and note. Not just from touching him —if in self-defense—and fighting his way out from under him more than once in that struggle. Not from the guilt and shame, from the way the cops had eyed him when asking Jack if it was true he'd been stalking him, as if assessing if he was a hot enough piece of ass to chase all the way from Vegas.

Everything, together, made him feel dirty.

When they finally caught their breaths after the door closed and River went to get them water, and Zeph approached him at the counter, River held up a hand before he could even speak. "Not yet."

Zeph hesitated, then nodded slowly and took his glass of water to chug it in a few quick gulps. "When?"

"Just wait. I need a shower."

Zeph looked relieved, and then contrite. "Of course. Sorry. I'll…" He waved vaguely at the living room. "Unless you'd rather I left? But I want to say this first."

"Don't you dare leave after all *that*," River whispered. Zeph gave him a quiet smile and reached out to touch his arm, then took his empty water glass. He hadn't realized he was still holding it.

"Go shower."

It was all he'd needed. River blinked back the tears of gratitude and nodded, trying to unknot everything that was tight and hot in his chest. He strode for the bedroom and shut the door, stripped, and hit the shower in record time.

With the hot water running down his body, blasting against his scalp and rinsing his face, he started to feel more grounded. More *present*, and human. Gradually, the exhaustion lifted, making it easier to sort through his thoughts.

Of course Zeph had come here for a reason, not just magically knowing Jack was there. River was almost positive Zeph was here to talk about their relationship.

What was that? Anger?

Yeah. He was angry at Zeph. River rolled his head back, letting the water stream down his face before he blinked and twitched free of the stream to gasp a breath.

He let himself own the emotion, let it fill his chest and tighten his body, and then fade slowly, washing down to the back of his mind, down his body, down the drain.

Hearing those things from him had hurt. Nic and Kyle were both right—he wasn't justified in saying, even if he hadn't outright, that he didn't care about him, or that they were better off apart. And River was so damn tired of teaching men how to handle their feelings, having random hookups dump their feelings on him like he was their mother just because he wore a damn skirt sometimes.

But Zeph wasn't doing that on purpose, because he was too manly to have feelings and he wanted someone else to handle them for him. Zeph was approaching him like this not because of who River was, but because of who Zeph was.

River drew a breath and let it out. Zeph didn't know exactly how to figure out how he felt, and he was quick to anger, and he was very quick to get scared, and shut down, and hide his feelings. River had known that for a long time— since their last relationship.

It didn't mean he didn't care. In fact, Nic and Kyle's words the other day had shaken River up. He hadn't real- ized that he was afraid of loving Zeph, but when it was put like that to him... Yeah. It was scary. And River was starting to suspect that Zeph feared how much he cared, too.

Didn't mean he wouldn't tell him what an asshole he was being when he was being one, but still.

By the time River got out of the shower, he was feeling calm and ready to talk. He dried off and found a fresh t-shirt and jeans before he came out and plopped on the couch next to Zeph.

Following pure instinct, River drew a breath and leaned into Zeph's side, taking his hand between his own. "Go."

"Uhh." Zeph blinked, caught off-guard, and then he gave River one of those beautiful, crooked smiles. "Makes it hard to think when you do that."

"I'm not sorry." River winked. "Makes it hard to rely on your usual brick wall of manliness."

Zeph closed his eyes as he laughed richly, then opened them again and looked at River. "You're a goddamn miracle, you know that?"

"I'm aware," River stuck out his tongue, then pulled up a knee to shift sideways and look at him. "But that doesn't sound like an apology, and I'm fairly sure I'm owed one."

"Yeah." Zeph drew his breath and laced his fingers with River's. "I'm sorry. What I said the other day... I was scared, and you're right. God, were you ever right. I started being stupid, and thinking about things, and I got so afraid of hurting you."

"So you hurt me, to keep from hurting me. Genius."

Zeph blinked, then nodded. "Yeah. I know, right? I'm... If you're willing to try it with me, I *want* to try to make it up to you. I can do better than that. I want to. Uh, I have no idea what I'm doing, but... I've never wanted to make it work so badly. And you know when I find something I really want, I'll work my ass off for it."

That sounded like a good apology to River, but Zeph wasn't done.

"And I found that thing, and it turned out to be you."

Zeph was nervously licking his lips. He'd never been this nervous—not before the fight, not before a show, or even when he'd asked River out the very first time. That was adorable.

River's lips tugged into a slow smile. "You want me to forgive you before or after the sex?"

"B…Before?" Zeph eyed him like it was a trick question.

"Damn. We'll save the hate sex and the make-up sex for next fight, then."

"Next… fight?"

River offered a grin. "Yeah. Next time you're an asshole, I'm not leaving the room until you admit it."

Zeph closed his eyes and groaned, but he was smiling anyway. "God. What have I gotten myself into?"

"I think the question is, what are you *about* to get yourself into?" River purred, walking his fingers up Zeph's thigh before he stood up and tugged open the button of his jeans.

As he walked, he slid down the zipper and started pulling his t-shirt off, keeping his pace to a steady saunter.

He didn't even have to look behind him to feel Zeph following him. To his bedroom, to his heart, to the very core of him and to his darkest fears, Zeph would follow. He might be clumsy and scared, but he was willing to own that now. River could work with that.

God, he was proud of him.

CHAPTER
Forty~Four

ZEPH

THERE WAS NOWHERE IN THE WORLD ZEPH WANTED TO BE more than in River's arms. Except maybe grinding up against him, both of them already naked as they hit the bed.

"You're such a tease," Zeph murmured, running his hands up River's back and kissing along his spine.

"I try my best," River beamed over his shoulder, then jerked his chin, prompting Zeph to lean in for a kiss.

"And so demanding."

"Another constant struggle," River sighed and flopped his head against the pillow.

"And cheeky."

"Mmhmm," River hummed. "I hope you appreciate all this effort."

Zeph slapped that perky little ass. "I sure do."

"Ooh! And *that* effort, too? I've been doing more squats lately."

"On my dick?"

River giggled. "And you say I have a dirty sense of humor?"

"That's cause you do." Zeph kissed River's top vertebra, then slowly worked his way down his spine, pressing slow, unhurried kisses along that sweet skin.

Hell wasn't a place for him anymore. It was just the path he was trying not to walk: running from his feelings, from the hard work of himself.

And to have the chance to do *this* every day—make River squirm and tremble with pleasure, make those tiny noises of pleasure spill from his lips? That was as close to heaven as he needed.

He grinned when he reached River's lower back and River gave a frustrated little moan. "Waiting for something?"

"Fucking tease. Good thing I love you."

"I love you, too," Zeph breathed. Then, he licked and kissed his way between those firm cheeks, along the opening and around it until the sensitive nerves had to be on fire.

River gasped and whimpered, pressing his body into the bed as his thighs twitched.

God, no matter what they did in bed from vanilla missionary sex to tying each other up with whipped cream and goddamn rimming, Zeph was satisfied. How one man had worked his way into his heart one no-strings-attached fuck or saucy joke at a time, he'd never know. He just knew he never wanted River to leave.

He slowly pushed his tongue inside the tight rim, then brushed his lips around the outside again, licking his way slowly down the perineum until he teased his balls. All soapy from River's shower just minutes ago, but he could live with that. As long as he got to wash the taste away with River's sweat when, later, he got him so turned on he was vibrating out of his skin.

"Gonna drive me nuts," River whimpered.

"Good."

"Gonna come too fast."

"I'll just make you come again." And Zeph meant it—if he had to wait until River was hard again, he could kiss him from head to toe and learn every damn sensitive nerve ending in his body in the meantime.

River whimpered under his breath, his knees digging into the bed. "Yes, *please.*"

Even from this angle, he could tell that River's dick was hard. He nudged him onto his side and shifted his weight to lie on his side next to him, head between River's thighs. He slowly kissed the side of the velvety shaft, then wrap his lips around the head, playing with his hole with two fingers while he sucked the shaft into his mouth and all the way down to his throat.

There was only so much he could take: feeling the hot skin pressing against him, every twitch of the muscles under his hands; smelling River's sweet shampoo; tasting the mix of salty precum and soapy skin; hearing every whimper and breathed utterance of his name; but most of all, seeing River's body spread on the bed for him, tight with pleasure, chest heaving. He was hard now, but he didn't stroke himself yet. He wanted to save every fucking moment for River's gorgeous little ass.

"F-Fuck," River whispered, clenching around his fingers. "Jesus *fuck!*"

Zeph closed his eyes, pushing River onto his back now so he could get a better angle, crouched above him, bobbing his head slowly first, and then faster. He tightened the suction, pulling in his cheeks and flicking his tongue the way he thought River did to him.

River was already whimpering with pleasure, his toes curling. "Babe, I'm… you'd better not."

Zeph pulled his head slowly up and licked the tip while he whispered, "You know I'll swallow."

"No," River whispered. "Not yet."

Zeph pulled away, kissing the tip once and eyeing River. "What?"

"Shut up," River breathed out, his lips tugging into a slow smile. "I just want my first orgasm with my boyfriend inside."

"You romantic," Zeph teased, but was he ever happy to oblige. He was already aching with need, so it only took a quick smear of lube across his hand and shaft before he was inside.

"No, I'm not," River retorted. "Just greedy."

"Uh huh." Zeph winked, moving his hips in a slow, steady rhythm at first to ease every inch of him inside. "I'll let you believe that."

River breathed out, "Sure. Nothing says romance like *I want you coming so much in me tonight that I'm wet for days.*"

Zeph *knew* River was trying to get a reaction, but he couldn't help the blush that washed across his cheeks. They burned despite himself. "Sounds like our kind of romance."

"Yeah." River's gasp when Zeph bottomed out and slammed into him again was mixed with a moan toward the end, so Zeph repeated it. "*Yes!*"

"Oh, yeah," Zeph growled, pushing into him hard and fast now.

River grabbed both of his hands and pulled them to either side of his head, then laced their fingers.

Zeph felt exposed suddenly, even though he was on top, driving into River hard and fast. When River looked at him like this, it was like his fucking soul was bare, and he had nowhere to hide.

But he didn't want to hide. He wanted River seeing and feeling every bit of him as River wrapped around him, as Zeph pushed into him, whichever it was… both at once.

"I love you," River breathed out and used their interlaced hands to haul his head down for a kiss.

Zeph's lips pressed hard against River's, and their tongues slid against one another's as their hands dropped to the bed again. His body slid against Zeph's, hot and sweaty already, his hard cock trapped between their stomachs, but he was whining with need like he was close to the edge already.

God, he was fucking beautiful, and Zeph wanted him to come so damn hard. But when he tried to pull his hand back, River wouldn't let go.

"Let me get you off."

River's voice was breathy, reedy. "I'll come like this," he promised. "J-Just like this. Fuck, baby. *Yes!*"

Zeph pressed his knees into the bed to anchor himself so he could thrust harder, deeper, while he kissed every curse word off River's mouth. His own body was throbbing and tightening, and with the most sensual sight in the world right in front of his eyes, no wonder.

River rolled his head back and bared his throat. "Baby, *so* close… oh, fuck. Please, yes, Zeph…" Words were spilling from his lips faster than he could form them, coming out as senseless noises as his hips started to rise off the bed, his back arching. "Y-You're so fucking perfect in me."

"You're the sexiest fucking man I've ever known," Zeph breathed out against River's throat, pressing kisses along the sensitive spots, all the way to behind his ear.

He'd just reached that spot when he found the magic angle, or when River just couldn't hold out any longer.

Either way, River's body tensed hard around him and then he cried out, his body clenching and quivering in rhythmic waves of fucking gorgeous muscle pressing up against him.

They always said you'd know love when you saw it, and Zeph had never known a moment like this: watching his lover come utterly undone under his own lips, burying himself with every thrust to the base of his shaft in him, smiling like there was no tomorrow.

The tightness around him made it impossible to hold out. It took just a couple more thrusts before he was there, too, his fingers squeezing River's hard as he gasped River's name into his neck and collapsed on top of him for a few last, hard thrusts.

Spilling every fucking last drop of himself inside, the way River wanted, but also pressing himself against River like he wanted to lose himself utterly in this man for every moment of his life.

Their grips loosened on each other's hands as they came down from the sex, but neither of them let go even as they lay together, softening and cooling off and regaining the ability to speak.

"Not bad, for a first orgasm," River finally announced. "I'll grade subsequent ones on a bell curve."

Zeph laughed until he couldn't breathe, and after a few moments, River joined in.

When they finally unlaced their hands, his hands were numb, but he still kept River pulled against his front.

"Feels like we can do this," Zeph admitted at last.

"Fuck all night long? If your dick won't break off, we can try," River agreed.

Zeph laughed. "Us, you. I mean *us.*"

"I know." River pressed his lips against Zeph's cheek and neck.

"I'm ready to try this… real relationship thing. Work on myself. Talk about shit, and… stuff," Zeph murmured, closing his eyes as River snuggled into his side.

River chuckled gently. "And I'll try not to push stuff at you when you aren't emotionally ready for it."

"No," Zeph murmured, cracking his eyes to peer at River before he pressed their lips together softly, just because he couldn't help himself and those soft, beautiful lips were right there. "No, that's when you do need to push me. I see what you have: your friends, your… your optimism. The way you love the world. The way you see it. I want that. I want to let people in."

River was gazing softly at him, his hands rubbing slowly along Zeph's chest and side. The touch was grounding, helping him form words. "Yeah?"

"I'm ready to try. I… I think I might want to make a difference for other people who've been hurt the way I have. I never told you about anything, really, did I?"

"You never had to."

"But I want to," Zeph told him. "You know when my parents died, I bounced around a bunch of foster homes? A couple of them were abusive. One in particular. And his brother was a priest who… well."

"Shit," River breathed out, his hand curling into a fist.

Zeph raised his hand to his lips, kissing those bruised knuckles until it relaxed. "Yeah. But I left the system as soon as I could, and then… Well. You know about Anton now, too. That was pretty big. I guess that's most of it."

"Okay."

Zeph eyed him carefully, checking for signs of freaking out, but River just gave him a small, knowing smile.

"I knew *you* long before I knew any of that stuff. You've let enough hints slip out. I love you for all your tangled past, and I'll keep loving you," River murmured, patting his chest gently.

"Oh." Zeph couldn't think of much more to say that wasn't *thank you*, and that sounded obnoxiously grateful somehow, so he just looked away and cleared his throat. "Right. Okay."

"But thank you for telling me officially." River cupped his cheek and pressed his lips against Zeph's again. "Put yourself first. You heal first, and then you can help heal others."

"I know. I'll work on it," Zeph promised. "But I think this would help me."

"Okay." River pressed his head against Zeph's shoulder and rubbed his chest again. "I'm proud of you."

"And I of you."

"Not just for beating down that Jack asshole?"

"Well, yeah. Mostly that. God, you're hot when you throw a punch," Zeph murmured with a grin at River.

It was River's turn to burst out laughing. "The way to a fighter's heart is through his knuckles, huh? Good thing it's not your stomach. Your meals are disgusting."

Zeph snorted with amusement and pulled River against him. "Shut up. You didn't mind my pre-fight meals."

"Yeah, I did. I totally pretended to like them."

"Liar."

River pecked his lips. "Uh huh. I'm secretly going after

your job." He flexed a bicep. "Can you see the difference already?"

Zeph wrestled River for that comment, letting him get on top when it became clear there were benefits to losing this match. Because when River was settled on his hard cock again, rising and falling at his own pace, he threw his head back and a mile-wide grin spread across his face.

Zeph was pretty damn sure he'd never known happiness like this.

"How'd the class go?"

"Great!" Zeph beamed as he strode into the gay and lesbian center, which had an office in the same building as Plus. He'd just finished up teaching a class for girls, women, and trans people in high-risk areas of the city.

Now, he was here to do the same lesson with a group of LGBT+ people, with the event cosponsored by Plus.

It was the third such class, and Zeph's confidence in teaching people had grown in leaps and bounds. Every time they offered it, they filled up too fast, so everyone planned to keep sponsoring as many sessions as possible.

It was also good business for Zeph's gym to be associated with him, and Zeph was working on organizing longer-term self-defense classes to offer to those who could afford to pay, which would subsidize other classes for those who couldn't.

His entrepreneurial spirit had come out of seemingly nowhere, along with his cheerier demeanor, as soon as he'd officially quit fighting. As he put it, he hadn't realized the toll it was taking on him.

Zeph still got up annoyingly early and ate gross food too often, but River could sneak more donuts and mac'n'cheese into his diet without feeling guilty.

And best of all, Zeph's courage had grown. He'd looked up his abusers before—both of the brothers—and found they'd just been thrown in jail. And Zeph had told him once, in a late-night unguarded moment, that if they applied for early release, he was prepared to go forward to petition against it. River had never, ever expected that of him.

"I'm so proud of you," River murmured, wrapping his arms around Zeph's waist and pulling him in for a slow kiss. He'd unpacked the mats already and set the place up for him, so as the attendees arrived, he stole a moment with him.

Not like anyone here, of all places, would complain. Not that Zeph seemed to care about that, either. Even when River was in a skirt and tights like today, he never hesitated to slide an arm around River's shoulders and tell the world with that trademark glare that he was his.

"There's some cuties here today."

A slight frown line formed between Zeph's brows. "There are?"

River loved it when he got all jealous. It made the sex later that much hotter. He barely stifled his giggle. "Uh huh."

"Don't think I don't know the game you're playing."

"Don't think I don't notice you're happy to play it, too. Especially when we get home and—"

"Oh, darling!" River was interrupted as RB came over, prodding their arms to get them apart. "Lord, give us three seconds without lip-locking."

Zeph obnoxiously kissed River again while River gave a muffled laugh.

"We're surrounded by them." That was Denver, setting up a table by the door with kits for each attendee—refresher pamphlets on what they'd learned, plus information from Plus. "Lovebirds."

"Like us?" Kyle's arms were looped around Nic's waist as he grinned, on his tiptoes so he could rest his chin on his shoulder.

"Them especially. They're worse," River declared.

Denver swapped a look with Tristan, who had turned up to learn more about the charity since he was considering publicly endorsing them.

"Uh huh," Tristan said. "Everyone's as bad as each other."

"Right?" RB clicked his tongue, fluttering his fingers toward the doorway as some of the queens arrived.

River smirked and pecked Zeph's cheek again. "You're just jealous."

RB squeezed one of Zeph's biceps. "Of that? I... suddenly lost my train of thought." He squeezed again. "Right... where was I?"

Denver cracked up in a snort-laugh, and then the others followed, unable to help joining in.

"I know, right?" River giggled. "And all mine."

"Look at him. All *boyfriended*." Kyle smirked obnoxiously. "You know, not so long ago, he was claiming he'd be single forever..."

"Oh, shut up," River scoffed, finally letting go of Zeph so he could go welcome attendees.

But it was true: how much his life had changed in a few short months.

His heart was light as he introduced himself and welcomed people, making sure everyone felt comfortable here. More than ever, he couldn't stop thinking about how lucky he was.

He's been telling me to look for love for years, but... Zeph wasn't around, or available, until now. River was convinced that there was fate, or at least very good timing, at work.

This happiness had been worth waiting for.

About the Author

E. Davies writes feel-good, low-angst romance that never fades to black when the going gets good! Born in Canada, after 16 moves and counting, Ed has finally put down roots in north London.

He emerges from his writing nest to coo over fuzzy animals, flee from cute guys, dance through the streets with his chosen family, put together fierce looks, and—most of all—befriend local flowers.

You can find all available titles at: www.edaviesbooks.com

FOLLOW E. DAVIES ONLINE:

amazon.com/author/edavies
bookbub.com/authors/e-davies
facebook.com/edaviesauthor
goodreads.com/edavies
instagram.com/edaviesauthor
x.com/edaviesauthor

Also by E. Davies

Sunrise Island Brothers:

Collide

Stranded

Hart's Bay:

Hard Hart

Changed Hart

Wild Hart

Stolen Hart

Significant Brothers:

Splinter

Grasp

Slick

Trace

Clutch

Tremble

Riley Brothers:

Buzz

Clang

Swish

Crunch

Slam

Grind

Brooklyn Boys:

Electric Sunshine

Live Wire

Boiling Point

F-Word:

Flaunt

Freak

Faux

Forever

Freedom

After:

Afterburn

Afterglow

Aftermath

Shared Universes:

Shelter

Adore

Miracle

Redemption

Limelight

Barely Regal